BEFORE WE SAY GOODBYE

Also by Toshikazu Kawaguchi

Before the coffee gets cold
Tales from the cafe
Before your memory fades

Toshikazu Kawaguchi

BEFORE WE SAY GOODBYE

Translated from the Japanese by Geoffrey Trousselot

PICADOR

First published 2023 by Picador
an imprint of Pan Macmillan
The Smithson, 6 Briset Street, London ECIM 5NR
EU representative: Macmillan Publishers Ireland Ltd, 1st Floor,
The Liffey Trust Centre, 117–126 Sheriff Street Upper,
Dublin 1, DOI YC43
Associated companies throughout the world
www.panmacmillan.com

ISBN 978-1-0350-2342-4 HB
ISBN 978-1-0350-2343-1 PB

Copyright © Toshikazu Kawaguchi 2021

Translation copyright © Sunmark Publishing, Inc. 2021

The right of Toshikazu Kawaguchi to be identified as the
author of this work has been asserted by him in accordance
with the Copyright, Designs and Patents Act 1988.

Originally published in Japan as SAYONARA MO IENAI UCHI NI
by Sunmark Publishing Inc., Tokyo, Japan in 2021
Japanese/English translation rights arranged with Sunmark Publishing, Inc.,
through Gudovitz & Company Literary Agency, New York, USA

3 5 7 9 8 6 4

A CIP catalogue record for this book is available from the British Library.

Typeset in Giovanni by Jouve (UK), Milton Keynes
Printed and bound by CPI Group (UK) Ltd, Croydon, CR0 4YY

Visit **www.picador.com** to read more about all our books
and to buy them. You will also find features, author interviews and
news of any author events, and you can sign up for e-newsletters
so that you're always first to hear about our new releases.

If you could go back, who would you want to meet?

Relationship map of characters

Woman in the White Dress

A ghost who occupies the seat that returns you to the past. She leaves to use the toilet once a day. Usually she is found quietly reading her novel. But she curses anyone who disturbs her.

Apollo

Golden retriever owned by Mutsuo and Sunao Hikita. He died last week, aged thirteen.

Miki Tokita

Baby daughter of Nagare

Mutsuo Hikita

He sometimes brought his dog Apollo into the cafe.

Mieko Kadokura

Wife of Monji Kadokura. Two and a half years ago she had an accident and fell into a vegetative state.

Nagare Tokita

Cousin of Kazu Tokita and owner of the cafe. He is a giant of a man, almost two metres tall. He has a baby daughter, Miki.

Sunao Hikita

Wife of Mutsuo Hikita and owner of Apollo. She regrets not staying awake with the dog when he died.

returned to the past

Monji Kadokura

An archaeologist and traveller. He has not spent much time at home with his wife and children.

returned to the past

Kazu Tokita

Waitress of the cafe Funiculi Funicula. She serves the coffee during the ceremony that returns people to the past.

returned to the past

Michiko Kijimoto

Six years ago she left home in Yuriage and went to university in Tokyo, partly to get away from her father.

returned to the past

Hikari Ishimori

Her boyfriend said he would wait for her when she turned down his proposal a year ago but then he met someone else and left her.

Fumiko Kiyokawa

Cafe regular whose boyfriend is in America.

Yusuke Mori

Fiancé of Michiko.

Nana Kohtake

A nurse and a regular of the cafe.

Yoji Sakita

He proposed to Hikari Ishimori in the cafe a year ago.

Kengo Kijimoto

Father of Michiko. He died in the Great East Japan Earthquake six years ago.

CONTENTS

I

The Husband

_____

'So, there's nothing one could do to change the present?'

Monji Kadokura inquisitively tilted his head of grey-speckled hair, dislodging a cherry-blossom petal that fluttered to the ground. Under the dim sepia light of the shaded lamps – the cafe's only illumination – he was squinting so closely at the jottings in his notebook that his face was almost pressed against the page.

'What does that mean, specifically?'

'Well, maybe I could explain it like this . . .'

Replying to Kadokura's question, with long narrow eyes, was Nagare Tokita, a huge man more than two metres tall. He was the owner of the cafe and always wore a white cook's uniform.

'Take this cash register, for example. You'd be hard-pressed to find one in Japan that is older. I've been told it's very rare.

By the way, even empty, it weighs forty kilograms, to stop people stealing it. Anyway, let's say that one day, this cash register *was* stolen.'

Nagare slapped his hand on the cash register on the counter.

'If that happened, then naturally you would want to return to the past and hide it away somewhere or get someone to stand guard to stop anyone from entering the cafe to steal it, right?'

'Sure, that makes sense.' Kadokura nodded in agreement.

'But you see, that can't happen. No matter how hard you tried to prevent the cash register from getting stolen, the thief would still make their way into the cafe and steal the cash register, even if it was well hidden.'

'Gosh, that is so fascinating. What could be the science behind that? I would be interested to know the causal relationship – if you know what I mean. A kind of butterfly effect, perhaps?' Kadokura looked up at Nagare with excited eyes.

'Butterfly effect?'

Now it was Nagare's turn to tilt his head, in confusion.

'It's a theory that the meteorologist Edward Lorenz proposed at a lecture given at the American Association for the Advancement of Science in 1972. There is a Japanese saying along the same lines. *If the wind blows, the barrel-makers prosper.*'

'Oh, er, OK.'

'But then, this idea of the present not changing – that's not an effect. More like a correction, don't you think? If so, that would rule out the butterfly effect. This is getting more and

2

more fascinating,' he mumbled enthusiastically as he wrote something down in his notebook.

'Well, truth be told, the only explanation we have ever been given is, *because that's the rule*, isn't that right, Kazu?' Nagare looked to Kazu Tokita, standing next to him, for agreement.

'Yes, that's right,' Kazu replied without bothering to look up.

Kazu was Nagare's cousin and a waitress at the cafe. She wore a white shirt, black waistcoat, and sommelier's apron. She was pretty with fair complexion and long, narrow almond-shaped eyes, but not one other feature stood out. If you glanced at her and closed your eyes, you'd find it difficult to describe her face. Even Kadokura had to follow Nagare's gaze to be reminded that there was one more person here. She cast a faint shadow, and her presence lacked impact.

Her expression remained neutral as she polished a glass.

Fumiko Kiyokawa cut into the conversation. 'So anyway, Professor Kadokura, who did you come to the cafe to meet?'

'Please drop the professor, Ms Kiyokawa. I'm out of academia now.' He smiled awkwardly and scratched his head.

Fumiko had already experienced a return to the past in the cafe: she went to meet a lover from whom she had parted ways. Now she was a regular and visited the cafe almost daily after work.

'Oh, do you two know each other?' Nagare asked.

'Professor Kadokura taught my archaeology class at university. But he's not just an archaeology professor. He has travelled around the world as an adventurer. As a result, his classes covered so much! I found them to be of great value,' Fumiko replied.

'You might be the only one who would say that. And I must say, you were an excellent student, always top of the class.'

'Don't talk me up so much . . . I simply didn't like losing to anyone.' Fumiko waved her hand modestly.

Notwithstanding how true that statement was, while still in high school Fumiko had mastered six languages through self-study, and she had graduated as the top student at her university. Her brilliance remained in Kadokura's memory even though he was no longer teaching. It simply wasn't true that she just hated losing.

'Professor, you never answered.'

'Oh yes, of course, you want to hear my story, right? Well actually . . .' Kadokura turned his gaze away from Fumiko, sitting next to him at the counter, and stared at his clasped hands. 'I want to see my wife . . . just to talk with her one more time,' he said in a small voice.

'With your wife? Oh, don't tell me she's . . .' Fumiko didn't need to finish the question. Her alarm told Kadokura what she meant.

'Oh, no, she's still alive.'

Kadokura's reply had softened Fumiko's expression. But his face stayed grim.

Sensing something was amiss, Fumiko and Nagare waited with bated breath for his next words.

'She's alive, but she suffered brain damage in an accident,

4

which left her in a vegetative state. It's been nearly two and a half years. Patients in a vegetative state normally survive three to five years at the most. I've been told that she is likely to die soon, considering her age.'

'I'm sorry to hear that. Then perhaps you were hoping to return to the past to prevent your wife's accident? If that was your plan, I'm sorry, but as I explained before . . .'

Shaking his head a little, he replied, 'No, I understand. I admit to a little wishful thinking, but now, to tell you the truth . . .' He scratched above his eyebrow. 'You've really piqued my interest,' he said and laughed nervously.

'What do you mean?' Fumiko asked, puzzled.

'I mean, the idea of not being able to change the present even though you can return to the past – how intriguing is that?'

His eyes shone like a child's, then darkened in an instant. 'That must have sounded rather inappropriate when my wife is in a vegetative state.'

'Oh, not at all.' Fumiko's attempt at a smile came off awkwardly. In truth, she had indeed thought, *How inappropriate.*

'That side of my personality caused my wife much distress. I've been in love with archaeology since my youth and I've lived a life focused on my interests alone. I trotted the globe as an adventurer and I did not return home for months on end. My wife never voiced any complaints about how I was. She tended to our home and raised our children. Then they left the nest, one by one, and before we knew it, it was just the two of us. Yet I continued to leave my wife alone and travel around the world. But waiting for me when I returned home one day was my wife – in a vegetative state.'

Kadokura took a small photo from his notebook. It showed a young couple. Nagare and Fumiko could see immediately they were Kadokura and his wife. After a longer look, it became plain that a large pendulum wall clock, looking just like one of the three in this cafe, was in the background.

'This photo was taken of us in this cafe, I want to say twenty-four, maybe twenty-five years ago. You've heard of an instant camera, right?'

'You mean an instax?' asked Fumiko in reply.

'People today call them that, yes. Cameras that could take photos and then allow you to print them on the spot were a hit back in the day. The lady in charge of the cafe back then had one. She took this photo for us, saying we should have a memento.'

'That was my mother. Mum loved having the latest in trendy gadgets. I imagine she said it was a memento, but I bet she just wanted to show it off,' said Nagare dismissively with a wry smile.

'My wife told me to carry this always. She said it was an amulet to protect me. Of course, there is no scientific basis for a photo to become a lucky charm,' said Kadokura as he waved the photo around.

'You want to go back to the day that photo was taken?'

'No. I haven't visited this cafe since that day, but I think my wife came here every now and then to meet our children. If I

6

return, I would like to go back about two or three years before she fell into her vegetative state.'

'OK then,' Nagare replied, and momentarily glanced over to the woman in the white dress with long black hair and pale skin that appeared almost translucent, sitting in the furthest corner of the cafe. She was silently reading a book.

'Do you have any other questions?'

'Let's see.' Kadokura put the photo back into his notebook and opened the page on which he had just jotted down the rules. Once again he brought his face close to the page as he peered at it.

'I think this is related to the rule that the present won't change, which we just discussed, but . . .'

'What is it?'

'How do words conveyed from someone from the future remain in the memories of the people they visit?'

'Eh? Well, that's, er . . .' Nagare could not grasp what Kadokura was asking. He knitted his brows and tilted his head. 'What do you mean?'

'Sorry, I'm not explaining this very well.' Kadokura scratched his forehead.

'I understand that there is some kind of force, which you call a rule, that works to prevent the present from changing. What I want to know is whether the rule has an effect not only on the present, but also on memory?'

A question mark still was hanging over Nagare's head.

'In other words, if people were told that the cash register

7

would get stolen, I want to know whether or not their memories would be erased or altered by the rule.'

'Ah, OK, I get you now,' said Nagare, folding his arms.

'And? What would happen?' butted in Fumiko instead of Kadokura.

'Well, let me think.' Nagare didn't have an answer straight away. That was because his mind went from, *I've never even thought about it,* to: *More to the point, what's on Kadokura's mind? Why does it concern him?* To the best of his knowledge, no one else had been bothered with such a thing before.

Now, siding with Kadokura, Fumiko stared inquisitively into Nagare's face as if she too was concerned about it.

Fumiko had once returned to the past to meet her boyfriend, from whom she parted at this cafe. Yet one other rule of this cafe was that after people have returned to the past once, they can never do so again. So this particular conversation shouldn't have interested her. Yet, here she was, coming at him as if she was Kadokura's sidekick.

New creases were appearing between his eyebrows, and Nagare wiped sweat from his forehead as his long thin eyes narrowed further. 'Um, let me think,' was all he could groan.

'Memories are unaffected by the rule.'

This snappy clarification was delivered not by Nagare, but by Kazu, who was next to him. She had finished wiping the glasses and was on to folding the paper napkins. Without the slightest pause, she imparted this crucial reply in a piercingly clear voice.

'There are cases where people know the truth, but in

conversations with others, act as though they don't know. They might learn that the cash register is going to be stolen. They might *know* it is going to be stolen, but still, they will approach that day pretending otherwise. The rule intervenes in that way. It operates through such pretence. It does not, however, interfere with people's memory. There is no case where a person forgets the experience. On the contrary, with the knowledge that the cash register will be stolen, that person spends every day worrying until the theft occurs. But how they perceive and live with that information is up to them. It all depends on how they take it. The memory and the emotions that arise from it belong to them. Those are outside the scope of the rule's interference.'

On hearing Kazu's explanation, Kadokura's expression brightened considerably. He stood up.

'If that's the case, then I'm glad to hear it. That's taken a load off my mind. I would now like to make a request. May I please return to before my wife fell into a vegetative state?' Then he bowed deeply.

'As you wish,' Kazu replied coolly.

Fumiko looked at Kazu and clapped loudly in applause, while Nagare looked utterly confounded. This was not a new rule, but a fact. It was hidden in the shadow of the second rule and brought to light by Kadokura's questioning. If you return to the past, the present will not change no matter how much you try. But there was a proviso: although the rule had power over any circumstances to prevent the present from changing, it did not interfere with people's memories.

Rather than concentrating his attention on the rule that the present would not change, Kadokura was concerned with the effect on memory. *Perhaps that's an important consideration.*

Glimpsing the profound implications of the rule, Nagare narrowed his long thin eyes still further as he looked up at the ceiling.

'Now, about the other rules . . .' Kazu said, resuming her explanation. But the other rules did not seem nearly as important to Kadokura. To the rules that you must not get up from the chair while in the past and that there is a time limit, he replied with a simple, 'Understood.'

However, when Kazu broached the topic of the woman in the white dress, mentioning that she was a ghost and that if you forcefully tried to move her you would be cursed, he devoured this information with a glow of childlike fascination in his eyes.

'Well, I still don't believe she is a ghost. But I must say, I do have a fascination with curses. In the world of archaeology, some uncanny stories are spread around as if they are true. And I have read many books on the supernatural. All of them, however, lacked scientific rigour. In fact, I've never met someone who has been cursed. I'd actually like to experience what it feels like.'

'What?' Fumiko shrieked. 'Are you serious?'

'Yes, of course. I'm very eager to try. Didn't you mention before, Ms Kiyokawa, that you had been cursed by her? I'm curious, how did it feel? Perhaps I too would get cursed if I tried to move her forcefully?'

Unsure what to make of Kadokura's conduct, Nagare and Fumiko looked at each other and shrugged. At the same time, Nagare thought, *He reminds me of Mum.*

Nagare's mother was also free-spirited and consumed by wanderlust. There was even a time when she called herself an adventurer. She pursued her interests voraciously, and as a result she had no regard for family. She was completely disengaged. Consequently, she and his father had divorced before Nagare was born.

After he was born, she left him in the care of her younger sister, Kazu's mother, while she moved overseas. He had heard that she was in Hokkaido, but as she just did as she pleased without letting anyone know her contact details, he couldn't be sure.

Mrs Kadokura had to put up with the same, no doubt.

Looking at Kadokura, who appeared to be as eccentric as his mother, Nagare couldn't help feeling a little sorry for his wife and children.

'Well, I think you would be able to experience getting cursed, but I definitely advise against it,' stated Nagare coldly.

Kadokura was unperturbed. 'But still, if possible . . .' he implored with an unnerving clarity of purpose in his eyes.

Oh no. There's no stopping him. I can't see him changing his mind whatever I say.

Nagare gave a mental sigh. 'Just this once, OK?'

'Thank you very much!'

As bizarre as he thought the situation was, Nagare still reluctantly ushered Kadokura over to the woman in the white dress. Kadokura nervously took out a handkerchief from his pocket. He stood next to the woman in the white dress while wiping the sweat from his forehead and hands.

'Excuse me, do you mind?'

Kadokura peered into the face of the woman in the white dress. The woman continued reading her book without responding or changing her expression in any way. Today she was reading a novel called *The Dog that Wanted to Be a Cat and the Cat that Wanted to Be a Dog*.

'Huh? She really . . .' Kadokura muttered as he stared at the woman's face.

'Is something wrong?'

'Er, no. Everything's fine. So, is it OK to force her to move?'

'Yes.'

'Right then, I'll get her to move.'

Kadokura took a deep breath and stepped up to the woman in the white dress.

'Excuse me, madam. Could I get you to move, please?' he said while shaking her shoulder.

The woman did not respond, so he looked to Nagare for advice.

'Try with a little more force.'

'Er, OK.'

With a sudden burst of decisiveness, Kadokura grabbed the woman's shoulder and yanked it firmly as he said, 'Excuse me! Please move!'

Suddenly, the woman in the white dress opened her eyes wide and glared at him.

'*Ugh.*'

Instantly, he buckled at the knees. The lights in the cafe flickered like candle flames, and from out of nowhere an eerie voice like a moaning ghost echoed throughout the cafe. The woman's pale white face transformed. Leaning over the table, she glared at Kadokura creepily with horrible round eyes.

'So, this is a curse! My body is so heavy, and . . . argh . . . it hurts too. I feel like my bones are being twisted. This is what a curse feels like! It's the first time I've experienced it! I feel so heavy, I can't move as I want. It feels like I am being covered by a blanket of lead. Ooh the heaviness!'

Kadokura was crawling on the floor with a look of pleasure.

'Is that enough?' Nagare asked.

Waiting there beside him was Kazu, holding a silver kettle.

Kadokura panted, 'Not yet, a little longer. I'm currently feeling what it's like to be cursed. An experience as precious as this doesn't occur every day . . .'

'If you say so.' Nagare sighed heavily.

From her counter seat, Fumiko looked down at Kadokura crawling on the floor and chuckled.

'Uh!'

It wasn't long before Kadokura's body was flat on the floor with his arms and legs splayed out. Strange indiscernible sounds, rasping from his throat, suggested he was struggling to breathe. He might have lost the ability to talk.

'Kazu,' said Nagare as a signal; he thought it dangerous to leave it any longer.

Kazu stepped up to the woman in the white dress, who was grimacing at Kadokura with wildly tousled hair. 'How about a fresh cup of coffee,' she suggested quietly.

In an instant, the woman in the white dress went from being on the verge of climbing over the table and attacking Kadokura, to saying, 'Yes, please,' docilely, as she sat down in her chair.

At the same time the cafe's lighting returned to normal and the ghost-like moaning vanished.

'Whew.'

The curse had been lifted. Kadokura recovered his ability to breathe. He was puffing hard, but he lifted his head to reveal an expression of childlike exhilaration.

The woman in the white dress sipped her coffee and quietly read her book.

'I see. I see. So that is a curse. How very interesting.'

In no time, Kadokura had picked himself up and returned to his counter seat, where he opened his notebook. He began writing something with remarkable speed.

Nagare was completely dumbfounded, while Fumiko was giggling like an amused bystander.

Kazu alone kept cool as if nothing had happened.

While Kadokura was engrossed in his notetaking, Fumiko suddenly said, 'Oh, Nagare, I was forgetting, how's little Miki? I came to peek at her face.'

Miki was the baby girl born to Nagare and his wife, Kei Tokita.

'What are you talking about? You saw her just yesterday.'

'Yes, I know, but . . .'

'How many times do you need to look at her?'

'What does that matter? She's so cute! I could look at her all day and not get tired.'

'That's a bit weird.'

Though his words didn't say it, his long almond-shaped eyes arched beamingly. He was happy.

'Is she asleep?'

'In the back room.'

'Can I see her?'

'Of course.'

'Thank you.'

Fumiko sprang up from the counter stool and grabbed her phone from her shoulder bag.

'Don't you think you've taken enough photos?'

'I want to take a video today.'

Grinning wickedly, she walked off into the back room.

'Are babies really that cute?' muttered Kadokura. He had finished writing in his notebook and was now looking towards the back room to where Fumiko had disappeared.

'Oh, I beg your pardon. I wasn't implying that your baby wasn't cute. I myself have two daughters and one son. They're all grown up now, and I even have grandchildren.'

'They weren't cute?' Nagare asked in disbelief.

'Well, I don't know. When my children were born, I was mostly overseas, you see. When I returned home each time they had always got bigger. My second daughter even said to me once, "Come and visit again sometime,"' replied Kadokura with a wry smile.

'Looking back now, I don't think I ever should have started a family. Before I knew it, they had grown up. By the time they were in middle school and high school, I didn't know how to interact with them. Even so, my wife did not say anything to me. She always sent me off with a smile.'

'Do you regret it?'

After pondering Nagare's question silently, Kadokura replied, 'Not having any regrets might actually be my biggest regret. I wish I was capable of feeling regret.'

Then he added, 'So what do I do now?'

'Huh?' Nagare's almond-shaped eyes widened momentarily. 'Er, that's not really something I can . . .'

'No, I mean to return to the past.'

'Oh, that.'

'Sorry, I confused you.'

'No, it's OK,' said Nagare, wiping a bead of sweat from his forehead.

'First, to travel back in time, you need to sit in the chair she is in, which means you must wait for her to vacate it. She always does once every day, when she goes to the toilet.'

'Are you saying she goes to the toilet even though she's a ghost? It just keeps getting more fascinating.'

'However, we don't know when she will go.'

'So what does that mean?'

'The only thing you can do is wait. If you try to force her to move, the same thing will happen as before.'

'She'll curse me.'

'Yes.'

'OK, I understand. May I order something to eat?'

'Yes, of course. If there's something not on the menu that you would like, I think I can make it for you providing we have the ingredients.'

'Oh, sounds good, may I have chicken and egg on rice?'

'You would like *oyakodon*?'

'Yes, long ago, my wife often made it for me. I would like to have that, please.'

'Sure, I'll go and make it,' Nagare replied and went to the kitchen.

That left Kazu, the woman in the white dress, and Kadokura. Kadokura opened his notebook again and started writing.

It feels quiet now.

It is normal for cafes to play classical or jazz music in the background. Customers can enjoy a cup of coffee while immersed in relaxing music. That is one of the pleasures of a cafe. Music was not played in this cafe, however. The only sounds were the three large, floor-to-ceiling pendulum clocks ticking away the time.

The time shown by each of the three clocks, though, was different. Checking his watch, Kadokura was able to confirm that the middle clock was the only one keeping the correct time. The times displayed by each of the three clocks, however, were completely different.

When some customers first visit the cafe, their sense of time goes a little haywire while sitting in the room with no

17

windows or sunlight. Re-immersing himself in this space now, Kadokura found his memory of his first visit to this cafe flooding back as if it was only yesterday.

'Actually, I've seen that woman before,' he said suddenly to Kazu, catching her unawares. 'It was when that photo I showed earlier was taken. I thought I was most likely mistaken. After all, it was twenty-four or twenty-five years ago.'

Kadokura looked at the woman in the white dress. Kazu was listening quietly to his story.

'But I'm not mistaken. It is her. She served me and my wife coffee here in this cafe that day. Her hair was a different length back then, but her sorrowful eyes are just the same. Why did she end up sitting in that chair? What on earth happened to her?'

Flap.

The sound of a book closing suddenly interrupted Kadokura's story. It was the woman in the white dress. She stood up slowly, then she moved silently past Kadokura's back where he was sitting at the counter and disappeared to the toilet.

Once she had gone, Kadokura turned round and looked at the empty seat.

'The seat is vacant now, right?'

'Yes.'

'If I sit on that chair, I can go back to the past?'

'That's right. Would you like to sit there?'

'Yes, of course.'

No sooner had Kadokura replied than he left the stool and stood in front of the chair that the woman in the white dress had been occupying – the chair that would take him back to the past.

Rather than immediately sitting down in the vacant chair before him, however, he stood staring at it.

It was a balloon-back chair with beautifully curved cabriole legs and a seat upholstered in a pale moss-green fabric. It was a replica, but still obviously worth a considerable sum.

Kadokura was no expert, but even he could tell that each of the chairs in this cafe was a high-class item worth several times the price of a normal chair.

However, it wasn't that which he was fixated on.

'It doesn't seem particularly different from the other chairs.'

Kadokura crouched down and stroked the seat cushion. He wanted to know whether this chair that took you back to the past was special in any way from the others.

'It's cold. More specifically, the space around the chair feels chilly. Why on earth would that be, I wonder? Perhaps it is this space that is special, and the chair is just the same as the others? I wonder if you could still go back if you switched it with another chair?'

He turned to see that Kazu was not there. He had been talking to himself. However, seemingly unperturbed, he carefully slid between the chair and the table.

'Yes. There's no mistaking it. It is obvious once you sit down. It's not the chair that is cool; it's this entire space that is chilly.'

Kadokura slowly moved his palm away from his body. He was using it to search for subtle temperature boundaries.

'From here . . . to here . . . to here . . . to here, the temperature is clearly different. It's just this space of about eighty centimetres long and wide that is special in some way; it begins from the middle of the table and includes the chair.'

Unbeknownst to Kadokura, Kazu had returned from the kitchen. Placed upon the tray she was holding were a silver kettle and a pure white coffee cup.

He spoke regardless. His tone remained the same whether Kazu was there or not.

'I am thinking perhaps it is actually this space of about eighty centimetres square that makes it possible to return to the past.

'Yes, that's right.

'I see. I see. How fascinating.'

Even now, Kadokura once again began to jot down something in his notebook.

While Kazu was clearing away the cup that the woman in the white dress had used, Nagare came out from the kitchen. He was holding a wooden ladle.

'Er . . .'

'Yes?'

'What do you want to do about the meal?'

'Oh, yes, I forgot.'

Kadokura had stopped writing and was looking up. He hadn't expected the woman in the white dress to vacate the chair so fast.

'Oh, what shall I do? Is it OK to wait until after I return?'

'Yes, of course.'

'OK, then when I get back.'

'Sure. No problem.'

Kadokura took a whiff of the air around him.

'That smells good, though. I'm looking forward to returning,' he said to Nagare.

'It will be waiting for you.'

Nagare's narrow almond-shaped eyes once again beamed with pleasure as he retreated to the kitchen.

'Right then . . .'

Kadokura sat up straight and gave Kazu a little nod. It was his way of indicating he was ready. Kazu stood silently at the side of the chair. When he looked at her face, a chill ran down his spine.

What a resemblance! She looks exactly like the ghost who was just sitting here.

He noticed it in her translucent complexion, her narrow eyes and pensive expression, and more than that, her bone structure – or rather, her silhouette. Perhaps it required the discerning capabilities of someone like Kadokura to notice it, but he felt certain.

They are mother and daughter.

Obviously, the woman in the white dress must be the mother and the waitress standing before him, the daughter.

I must know the story behind this.

But he held his tongue. Clearly aware of the immensity of having one's own mother become a ghost and permanently sit there, not ageing, he knew it was not a subject to be broached out of personal curiosity.

Nevertheless, I still want to know.

'I was wondering . . .'

No, I can't.

Mentally, he was vigorously shaking his head as if to sweep away the question crossing his mind.

Let's stick to going back to the past right now.

'Er, never mind. Please continue.'

When Kadokura looked up to Kazu, she placed the empty coffee cup before him immediately, as if she had been waiting for him to look at her.

'I will now pour the coffee.

'Your time in the past will commence once your coffee has been fully poured and it will last until your coffee gets cold.'

'Yes. I know.'

'When back in the past, you must remember to drink all your coffee before it cools.'

'Before it cools?'

'Yes.'

'Why is that?'

'If you don't drink it all up before it cools . . .'

'What happens then?'

'You will turn into a ghost and end up permanently sitting in that chair.'

'WHOA!' he shouted in the loudest voice heard today. Even when he was struck with the curse, he hadn't been as loud. It wasn't simply his surprise at hearing he would become a ghost if he didn't drink up all the coffee, his shout was all the louder because he'd realized that if that was true, he had solved the mystery of why the waitress he had seen long ago in the cafe had been sitting in the chair looking no different from back then.

It also confirmed his hypothesis that the waitress standing before him was indeed the daughter of the woman in the white dress.

What bizarre circumstances . . .

Kadokura looked at Kazu's face in a daze. 'Why did that happen to her?' he asked spontaneously. 'Oh, gosh. Sorry. Please forget I said that. Let's continue.'

He desperately tried to take back what he'd said. But he felt left high and dry, with no possible words that could save him.

Yet Kazu's complexion did not change. 'She . . . Kaname . . . went to see her dead husband,' she replied.

'Oh, gosh. Really?!'

To hear Kazu refer to her not as Mum, but by her name was crushing.

'She knew the cafe's rules well. But I guess she simply lost track of time. It must have slipped her mind until after the coffee went cold . . .'

'And that turned her into a ghost?'

'Yes.'

'I see,' Kadokura said, his forehead furrowing in reaction to the story.

That is heavy news.

All the rules on returning to the past that he had heard so far may have been inconvenient, but they weren't outright dangerous. Even if you cannot meet someone who has never visited the cafe, even if you can't get up from your seat, and even if you cannot change the present, none of those rules pose a risk.

He had learned first-hand what it was like to get cursed. It certainly was painful, but not unbearably so. Just as people have pressure points that hurt when pressed, it had felt like his pressure points were being stimulated.

Now, afterwards, he even felt refreshed with a renewed sense of clarity. In fact, after being cursed, his stiff shoulders, a cause of long-term suffering, had felt better. Perhaps it was a curse by name, but he thought it could even be considered as a therapeutic massage.

But this new rule was something completely different.

If I hadn't realized that she and the ghost were daughter and mother, I might not have fully appreciated how risky this rule is.

Kadokura had made up his mind on what he should say to his wife when he returned to the past. He didn't think it would take very long to say.

When told he could only stay in the past until the coffee got cold, it hadn't shaken him. He thought that sounded plenty of time. However, he had now realized the relationship between those two women. They were clearly mother and daughter.

What a cruel rule. Well, cruel for this mother and daughter, at any rate.

He inhaled one deep breath to allow his feelings to settle.

OK, it's time to focus on going back to the past, he told himself.

'So, I must drink all the coffee before it goes cold.'

'Exactly.'

'Fine, I understand. You may pour the coffee now.'

On hearing his words, Kazu slowly picked up the silver kettle in her right hand. Kadokura was mesmerized by her movement. She held the kettle up in front of her chest, blinked tranquilly, and performed every gesture elegantly and efficiently.

How beautiful. Kadokura exhaled spontaneously. Kazu kept her eyes cast down at the empty cup. Even Kadokura had noticed that the air was becoming pregnant with tension. The only sound was the three clocks ticking away.

Dong, dong, dong . . .

The far-left wall clock suddenly began chiming.

'Right then,' Kazu said, as if that was the signal she was waiting for, and then whispered, 'before the coffee gets cold.'

Her words reverberated throughout the cafe, and the already tautened air seemed to tremble with further intensity.

The space around me feels even cooler.

The coffee-pouring ritual continued. As if in slow motion, Kazu began pouring coffee into the cup.

Gosh . . .

As a plume of vapour rose from the filled cup, the entire eighty-centimetre-square space he was sitting in began warping and rippling in a dance with the undulations of this vapour.

The warping and rippling engulfed Kadokura, making him feel dizzy.

What on earth! Am I vaporizing?

Kadokura looked at his hands turning into a vapour. His gaseous body rose slowly.

His surroundings began flowing downwards.

I never imagined I could experience something so strange!

Kadokura gazed in delight at the scene. If only his vaporous hands were usable, he would have pulled out his notebook and jotted notes. He tried desperately to observe what was passing by him.

I would have brought a video camera if I'd known I'd see this!

And with that regret, his consciousness faded.

My wife Mieko was a quiet woman. She seldom spoke and held no opinions of her own. She was accepting of everything and intolerant of nothing. She had divorced once. The marriage with her first husband was the result of matchmaking. When I asked her why she divorced, she simply replied, 'He said I was boring.'

My marriage with Mieko was also the result of matchmaking. I was thirty-one, and Mieko was twenty-eight. Even at that age I was already deep into archaeology, and rarely at home in the apartment I was renting.

'Marriage with me will be impossible. I don't have money and I rarely come home. Who would want to marry someone like me?'

But despite telling that to my nosey matchmaker aunt, she still stubbornly set me up to meet Mieko.

Then Mieko said, 'I have no problem with all that.'

Yet, despite Mieko's assurances, I was sure she would soon hate me and want a divorce. I didn't think I could have a life-long companion. Not only was I obsessed with archaeology, but I also didn't care about anything other than what interested me.

I never imagined someone like me could ever make others happy, as I only ever thought of myself. I still think so. Yet Mieko never uttered the D word.

'See you later. Please take care.' Her words were few, but she always sent me off with a smile.

Then whenever I returned home after spending months away, she would welcome me back with something like, 'Oh, you're home. Do you want dinner?' She made it sound like I had just left that morning.

My love of conversation was greater than I thought. After returning from an expedition, I would have conversations with Mieko about things that happened at the dig, and what I saw and heard, which I had recorded in my notebook.

However, at the end of the conversation, Mieko would always finish with, 'All that stuff just goes right over my head.'

Nevertheless, she always would listen to my stories without interrupting me until I finished. I never cared if she understood what I was talking about. I think I just wanted someone to talk to.

I know I have a reputation in my circles as an eccentric. I think I was perhaps lonely. I had thought that it was OK to be lonely. And being as I was, Mieko was the only person ever to provide a place where I could feel at home.

After the kids were born, however, colleagues began suggesting to me, 'Why don't you spend more time at home?'

That caused me more stress than I had ever imagined. It stressed me because I had always considered myself someone incapable of intimacy. I hadn't even believed I could stay married.

It was working with Mieko because she was special. The kids, though, just wanted an ordinary family with a normal dad. But I couldn't change. So it was no shock to me when my second daughter said, 'Come and visit again.'

That was clever, I thought when she said it. I admired her sense of humour.

Luckily, my research was receiving recognition and we weren't in financial difficulties. When the kids entered adulthood, the only thing I could do was to buy them a house.

'Finally, you're doing something dad-like,' my elder daughter said, but I don't know whether you could call that *dad-like* when money was of no interest to me. I had no use for it.

I had simply taken Mieko's advice and used something that has no value to me to buy my daughter a house. When I asked whether I should buy Mieko a house too, she turned me down, saying, 'This apartment is all I need.'

So, she and I have been living in the same apartment for ever. For me, it's just a place I occasionally come home to. But even if it's just that, Mieko said it was fine.

If I had married any other woman, I doubt it could have

lasted. I wonder what Mieko's thoughts were on that. Now there is no way of knowing.

'Poor Mum.'

'You should treat her better.'

'She's all alone now.'

My kids worried about their mum, as kids do.

'If only you were a more normal dad.'

My son had said that when he was in elementary school. At the time, I had no idea what kind of father a normal dad was. I'm sure my kids, likewise, were unable to understand the happiness I was pursuing.

Yet even so, Mieko and I shared our lives. But Mieko had an accident and fell into a vegetative state. Her eyes no longer saw; her ears no longer heard. My children grieved, but as much as I felt it my place to grieve as well, I had no idea how to.

She was still alive.

When my expedition ended, I returned to the hospital room where Mieko lay. For me, home was where Mieko was, and nowhere else.

'I have to tell you all about the amazing things I discovered this time.'

Now when I went off into elaborate explanations, not only did she not understand but also my words no longer reached her ears.

She fell into the vegetative state about two and a half years ago. Her doctor told me, 'A recovery is not impossible, but considering her age, she could physically last for one year at best. Whether she can last another six months, I couldn't say.'

'I see. Thank you, doctor.'

For the first time in my life, I truly knew this feeling called *regret*.

As I had always stayed true to my passions, I always assumed that I would be free from unfinished business. But one point of unfinished business had arisen. I needed to return to the past and tell Mieko before she fell into a vegetative state *what I had forgotten to tell her*.

'Dad? Why are you here?'

My daughter's shrieking voice awoke me.

Cradling my granddaughter, she was staring at me from the cash register. I looked around, but nothing about the cafe was different from before I had returned to the past. It was still illuminated in a sepia hue from the shaded lamps. The wooden ceiling fan was rotating above. And the three large pendulum clocks were ticking away at their different times.

If my daughter hadn't been cradling my granddaughter, there was nothing to indicate I had gone back to before Mieko had fallen into a vegetative state. Before I went back to the past, my granddaughter was six.

She would enter elementary school next year. Then, as I looked at her sitting in my daughter's arms, she looked two or three. I must have gone back three or four years into the past.

But Mieko's not here.

It was a small cafe. Even from the furthest back corner, there were no blind spots. The only person I saw was the waitress who had poured my coffee, now standing behind the counter.

'Dad? Where did you come from?'

This time, it was my second daughter showing her face from behind my elder daughter.

'Huh?'

For a moment, my son stood in the doorway, but then he drew back. 'Hey, Mum. You're not going to believe this, but Dad's here,' he said.

My daughters, son and Mieko must have just arrived at the cafe together.

'Hello there!' said Mieko upon seeing me. She walked over and sat down in the chair opposite.

'Hello. Welcome,' said the waitress as she served glasses of water to everyone. Mieko ordered a coffee and my second daughter and son, sitting down at the middle table, ordered iced coffees.

My elder daughter remained standing beside our table holding my granddaughter.

'I will have a lemon squash, and could I have a lukewarm milk for my daughter? We'll have them at the counter,' she said to the waitress.

'Of course,' the waitress replied with a courteous nod, and left for the kitchen.

'You should have told us you were coming.'

'But didn't you say you were going to a dig in France?'

'Mum, did you know that Dad was coming?'

Responding to this to-and-fro from my daughters, Mieko shook her head.

France, that means it must be some time around June, three years ago.

By piecing my memories together, I worked out roughly when this day was. Mieko had had the accident that caused her to fall into a vegetative state around Christmas, about six months after this time.

According to my daughters, Mieko had been walking along a pavement when someone on a bicycle – while texting – crashed into her.

Despite falling and hitting her head badly, she managed to pick herself up and return home as if nothing had happened. However, she suddenly lost consciousness and fell a second time in front of our apartment.

A neighbour called 119 and she was carried off in an ambulance. She never regained consciousness.

It was so sudden.

A persistent vegetative state is a disorder of consciousness. The cerebrum gets damaged, and thinking, seeing, hearing, and purposeful actions are lost. But the brainstem's functions that control breathing and other vital functions for staying alive are preserved.

In contrast, a person who is brain dead has no brain functions and breathing is impossible without a ventilator.

In their case, life won't persist beyond two weeks even with a ventilator.

However, a coma can continue from two to five years, depending on the person's condition.

There was a woman in the United Arab Emirates who woke up twenty-seven years after falling into a coma.

They said they don't expect Mieko to last much longer, given her age . . .

It would probably be unfathomable to Mieko, now sitting in front of me, that she would fall into such a state. Even if I were to tell her then to avoid the accident, it still would not be possible to change the present.

I understood that.

But, *what if . . .*

Nothing is set in stone in this world. Perhaps there is a loophole in the rules, and the actual timing of Mieko's accident can change? I don't think it would be totally impossible. Yes, the timing of the accident could change, maybe by a year, or two – or five, or ten. The present where she has fallen into a vegetative state might not be changeable. But still, maybe the time of occurrence can be adjusted?

Two choices arose in my mind.

I should believe the rule and say what I want to say to Mieko. I shouldn't tell her about the accident as it would cause unnecessary stress for Mieko and the kids.

That was my initial thought.

I should consider the possibility there might be a loophole in the rule. I should tell Mieko what I want to tell her but just in case, I should tell her about the accident too.

33

If there was even the slightest possibility, I wanted to try to change the timing. However, the waitress had said, 'There is no case where the person forgets the experience.' Those words were weighing heavily on my mind. If I were to tell them about the accident and Mieko falling into a vegetative state, they would have to live with that knowledge. The more I thought in circles, the more I felt like I was stuck in a maze without an exit.

'Dad, isn't this the first time you have seen your granddaughter?'

'It would be pretty awful if that was true.'

'We are talking about Dad here, it's not impossible.'

'Come to think of it, sis, it doesn't look too good on you, either, if you can't remember.'

'I guess it doesn't. But hey, this is Dad we're talking about, he's seldom even in Japan.'

'That's true.'

'When you were a kid, you said to Dad, "Come and visit again sometime," do you remember?'

'That was Takeo, wasn't it?'

'Was that Takeo?'

'It wasn't me. I was the one who said, "Who are you, Mister?"' my son cut in.

'So "Come and visit again sometime" was me? I don't remember.'

'By the way, Takeo, Mum said your second child was born?'

'Yes, last month.'

34

'It's a shame you didn't bring him along. It's a rare opportunity to get Dad to see him.'

'That's true. If I had known, I would have brought him.'

'Why didn't you let us know you'd be here?' my elder daughter suddenly asked me.

I was still undecided whether I should tell them about the accident. I knew Mieko well enough to feel certain that she would accept the news calmly. That was how she was. If she wasn't like that, she would not have remained my wife until today.

The problem was my children. Imagining that such shocking news would leave them distraught, I told an arbitrary lie.

'I forgot some important documents. I arranged to meet Mr Kumada here to pick them up.'

I shouldn't decide just yet. I should wait and see.

That was what a voice of caution inside my mind was saying. And I agreed with it. I should wait a little longer and see.

However, my elder daughter did not accept my reasoned lie. 'Even if it's a lie, you should at least say you're here because of the wedding anniversary,' she said unexpectedly.

I couldn't connect the dots. It came out of nowhere.

'Wedding anniversary? Whose?' I cocked my head.

'You've got to be kidding? You came without knowing?'

'Seriously?' Both my elder and second daughters gaped at me incredulously.

'Don't you know it's the wedding anniversary that brings Mum to this cafe every year?'

'Why would your mother feel the need to come to this cafe every year for someone's wedding anniversary?'

'Moron,' my elder daughter sighed in an exaggerated way and sat down on a counter stool.

Mieko chuckled softly.

'Mum, how can you not be angry?'

'Oh, come on, I think it's expected for Dad,' remarked Takeo.

'What? You mean to have us all seething?'

'Agreed.'

My elder and second daughters drank their lemon squash and iced coffee and loudly plonked their glasses on the table in anger.

'So, whose wedding anniversary are you talking about?'

'Right, that's it. Mum, let's leave.'

'If he were my husband, I would have already divorced him. Unbelievable.'

My daughters turned their angry red faces away from me.

'Please explain what's going on.' I turned to my son for support.

My mind was still stuck on whether I should tell her about the accident, and I couldn't pay attention to something I had no personal knowledge of.

My son rose from his seat and stepped between his sisters, gesturing to them to calm down.

'Dad, you probably have forgotten, but twenty-something years ago, you visited this cafe, right? With Mum.'

'Yes, we visited. Once only.'

'And wasn't that day your wedding anniversary?'

'Was it?'

'Yes.'

'Our wedding anniversary?' I cocked my head again.

'It's *your* wedding anniversary!' said my eldest savagely.

'Then why must Mum come to this cafe every year?'

'Better to ask Mum, don't you think?'

My son shrugged and my two daughters sighed heavily.

When they looked at Mieko, she smiled bashfully. 'Ha-ha. I just came on my own whim.'

I never understood the feeling of cherishing a wedding anniversary. And I think only Mieko understands that side of me. My kids would be happier if I embraced social norms. But I have never seen the value in them.

'Oh no . . .'

The cup in my hands had cooled more than expected.

That's something I can't forget. I must drink the coffee before it gets cold.

I took a sip of the coffee.

Lukewarm.

This talk about the wedding anniversary had prevented me from beginning the conversation. I had to decide quickly whether to tell her about the accident or not.

'Oh!'

Suddenly, I noticed the waitress standing quietly behind the counter.

Why didn't I think of that earlier?

I raised my hand and called to her, 'Excuse me, may I ask a question please?

'I know the present is set in concrete, but perhaps the exact timing of things leading to that outcome is not. Is it possible such timing could shift a little?' I asked, getting straight to the point due to the precious little time left.

My kids must have been befuddled by what I just said.

They still hadn't caught on that I had come from the future.

But I thought the waitress would understand my question, considering she worked at this cafe.

As expected, she replied simply with, 'I couldn't say for sure.'

That was good enough for me.

OK. I've made up my mind.

'I'm sorry about the wedding anniversary,' I said. 'I didn't know it was my wedding anniversary. I remember the day you mentioned. It was one of those rare days I had some free time, and Mieko suggested, "Why don't we go somewhere?" and I said, "OK, let's go to a cafe," and that's why we came here together . . . I'm just a bad husband who doesn't remember wedding anniversaries. Mieko, I hope you can forgive me for that. That's it.'

My daughters each looked at me with my head bowed, then looked at each other. They cast their eyes down, no doubt uncomfortable at the unexpected sight of me bowed low.

The awkward silence was saved by Mieko.

'I don't mind. If I know anything about you, I know you

have no interest in wedding anniversaries,' she said with a chuckle.

She reacted just as I thought she would. Mieko was that kind of woman.

'The truth is, I came from the future for a reason.'

'What?' My downwardly gazing daughters both raised their heads at once.

'Then, the rumour about this cafe—'

'It's true. Yes,' I confirmed, cutting off my son short with my hand.

It would be easier to get to the point if everyone had an inkling of what was going on, but there was no time to listen to that talk.

'In about six months, Mieko will have an accident and fall into a vegetative state. She will stay like that for two and a half years,' I said, choosing to bet on the possibility.

'A vegetative state?'

'Yes,' I replied succinctly to Mieko's question.

'Oh gosh,' Mieko mumbled, looking down with understandable shock.

'You're kidding, right?'

'What are you saying? That's not funny.'

Both my daughters were glaring at me incredulously.

My son, though, looked like his heart had sunk. He must have been familiar with the cafe's rule: the present cannot be changed.

'Believe me or not, I'll leave that up to you.'

'How could you say such a thing?' my elder daughter cried with a shriek that resounded throughout the room.

Alarmed by her voice, my granddaughter burst out crying.

Yet even with her beloved daughter crying in distress, my elder daughter's yelling continued unmoderated.

'I know about this rumour. I had never thought about whether it was true. But even if it is true, what a nerve! Have you any idea what you just said to Mum? In about six months . . . what? And you just say it so matter-of-factly, without changing your expression. How could you?'

'Just listen, there's no time.'

'I couldn't care less! You've always been like that! It was never about anyone but you! You never ever considered Mum's feelings, or ours! You always have us wrapped around your finger. I've had enough. Why do you do this? You should at least consider Mum's feelings.'

After saying all that, my elder daughter sat back down on the stool, exhausted. My granddaughter in her arms was crying. But she had no composure left to comfort her.

My second daughter took my granddaughter from my elder daughter's arms. 'Are you saying there is no way to avoid the accident that Mum gets into?' she asked coolly.

'It's unavoidable,' I replied tersely.

'So why did you come? You didn't just come here to inform Mum of her inevitable fate, did you?'

'Er, no . . .'

'Well then, just wrap it up. Say what you want to say and

get out of our sight.' Her tone was calm, but she clearly remained angry at what I had reported.

Still, I was inwardly relieved. *Thank heavens*, I thought. The coffee's temperature passing to my hands was telling me I had little time remaining.

'Fine.' I had no regret that I had foretold the future.

But if I were to return without doing anything else, my actions would be in vain. Now was not the time to consider what was good or bad. I had to make sure what I had told them was not pointless. That was the most important thing.

'Mieko.'

'Yes?'

'Until now, I have lived my life as I wanted to live it.'

'Yes.'

'I did what I wanted to do at all costs.'

'Yes.'

'I therefore thought I had no regrets in my life of sixty-seven years.'

'I'd think not.'

'That was until you fell into a vegetative state.'

'Oh goodness.'

Mieko looked at me in total surprise.

'I was surprised too. It was the first time I realized it. That I did have regrets. It was the first time I felt that way. But I cannot talk to you in the future about anything. That's why I came. There is something I want to say to you.'

'To say to me?'

'Yes.'

'OK, I'm listening.'

'I was happy in my life with you.'

Those were the words that I had regretted I could not say to her.

Once Mieko had fallen into a vegetative state, I could talk to her, but I couldn't tell her anything.

'I've never said anything like this before, so you might not believe me. I wanted you to know that I was happy *because* of you. I wanted to tell you. I *was* happy. Thank you. That's all I wanted to say.'

And with saying that, I drank down my coffee in one go. It was more bitter than the coffee I was used to drinking. Its sharpness seemed to perk me up while its aroma permeated deeply into my nose. My throat felt no warmth from swallowing it. The coffee had been perhaps only a few seconds away from going cold.

That was a close one.

I found myself putting the cup back down on the table and inhaling deeply. I looked at my daughters, who were looking back at me in dismay. They looked to be struggling to keep up with the wild conversation we had just had with its roller-coaster ups and downs.

'Don't be perturbed by what I said.' My granddaughter was now sleeping in my second daughter's arms. 'Just think of it this way: your mother will fall into a vegetative state in about six months. The accident happened so suddenly, it found everyone unprepared.

'When it happens, any regrets such as mine, like I should

have done this, or I should have said at least this, will be too late. Whatever you say, the rule will ensure that your mum will fall into a vegetative state. It is unavoidable. But your memory of what happened today will remain with you.'

I was getting dizzy, and my surroundings were beginning to undulate.

'That is why you need to treat your mum well for the next six months so that there are no regrets. Even better than before. You do that for me.'

'OK . . .'

As I thought I heard my second daughter's voice, my body was suddenly turning to vapour and beginning to rise towards the ceiling.

'Dad!' my elder daughter screamed.

I could see the tears welling in her eyes.

I could not tell whether they were from anger or sadness.

My surroundings were flowing down around me.

At that point, I was beginning to black out.

As I was fading, I suddenly noticed Mieko looking up at me. She too was crying.

'Mieko!'

'Darling.'

'I won't say goodbye.'

I was still holding out for the possibility for a shift in the timing. I wouldn't know for sure until I returned to the future.

'I . . .'

'Yes?'

'I've always been happy.'

'Oh, really?'

'Yes.' Mieko's voice was just as beautiful as ever.

Upon his return from the past, Kadokura chose not to eat the *oyakodon* chicken and egg on rice, and instead left the cafe in a rush.

He caught a taxi to the hospital where Mieko lay.

The window of the hospital room was open, and the white lace curtain was billowing in the breeze. A photo of their children was on the desk beside Mieko's bed.

Kadokura stepped silently into the room and hung up his spring coat while catching his breath. A cherry blossom petal that had latched onto it fluttered to the floor.

'The timing didn't change . . .' Kadokura said as he sat down beside the bed.

Mieko's chest gently rose and fell. 'How strange,' he said, voice trembling, as he continued watching her breathe.

'I managed to get rid of my regrets. But now I'm hoping that you will wake up!' Tears rolled down his cheeks. Many times, he tried to wipe them away. But those persistent tears would not stop.

II

The Farewell

'Your dog?'

Nana Kohtake, sitting on a counter stool, tilted her head to one side and raised an eyebrow. She worked at the local hospital as a nurse. It had become her daily routine to drop into this cafe after work.

'Yes, his name was Apollo,' replied Mutsuo Hikita, removing his rain-wet glasses.

Mutsuo was thirty-seven years old. He had a crew-cut and a beard. He was wearing a polo shirt and half-length trousers, and holding a backpack. He stood at the entrance looking soaked.

'It's raining? The forecast said it would be fine today.'

Nagare Tokita came out from the back room holding a towel.

'Thanks,' Mutsuo said, taking the towel gratefully.

'Yes, you sometimes brought him when you visited the cafe, the golden retriever, right?'

'Yes. That's the one.'

'Did something happen?' Nagare asked, which caused Mutsuo's expression to darken.

'Yes, he died last week of old age. He was thirteen.'

'Oh dear. That's sad to hear . . .'

'Yeah, well . . . it wasn't too bad for him. I think he might have passed away without suffering,' Mutsuo replied while wiping his wet head with the towel.

'Might have?' Kohtake queried.

'Ah, I mean . . . in his last moments, my wife . . .' Mutsuo choked up. After a silent pause, he finally inhaled determinedly and looked up.

'Apollo was our pet, but for his thirteen years, he had been really special to us as a couple. We wanted to have kids, and even tried fertility treatment, but it hasn't been possible, you see . . .'

'Well, I guess thirteen is pretty good for a dog. That's close to ninety for a human, isn't it? It's actually quite long for a big dog like a golden retriever, right?' said Kohtake gently, looking straight at Mutsuo's sad face.

'Yes, it is. So, we were both prepared. For the last few days before he passed away my wife and I took turns, constantly tending to him, so as not to leave him alone. We never thought of it as a chore. In fact, we cherished every day we had together and wished it would continue. We wanted him to live even one second longer. That was the only thing on our minds.'

46

While listening to Mutsuo, Nagare's eyes were fixed on a photo in a frame placed on the side of the cash register: a smiling Kei Tokita. His expression did not change. 'I know what you mean,' he said simply, as if to himself.

'Finally, after Apollo's temperature dropped and he started spasming now and then, my wife stayed by his side, mostly going without sleep. But because of that . . .'

'Oh no . . .' Kohtake and Nagare exchanged looks.

'Yes. It was when just my wife was with him. She woke up to find Apollo had gone cold.'

'But . . . such things . . .'

'Yes, I know. Such things can't be helped. I told her that too. But my wife can't forgive herself for falling asleep. She was unable to say goodbye at the very end.'

'So, in other words, it's *your wife* who wishes to go back to the past?'

'Er, not exactly.' Mutsuo shook his head. 'My wife still doesn't know about that aspect of the cafe.'

'Then what are you saying?'

'It's just that . . . if it was possible to return to the past, and see Apollo's face one more time . . . I thought it might cheer her up . . .'

'I see.' Kohtake nodded and slurped the last drop of her iced coffee.

Nagare was listening to Mutsuo with his arms crossed.

'You do know there are rules for going back to the past?' he asked.

'Yes ... I read about the rumour of the cafe in this magazine.'

'Magazine?'

In an affront to Kohtake's disbelieving eyebrows, Mutsuo pulled out a magazine from his backpack.

'What's that?'

'Oh, you haven't seen this?'

Kohtake shook her head as she flipped through the magazine. With Kohtake still holding it, Mutsuo turned a few more pages and pointed to an article.

'There, read that.'

'*The truth about the urban legend of the cafe that can take you back in time.* What is this?'

Kohtake looked at Nagare, surprised.

'Oh, some journalist came around long ago. Gosh, how many years? Kazu was still in junior high school ... so seven or eight years ago.'

Kohtake looked at the magazine again.

' "The cafe's name is Funiculi Funicula. A rumour that it can take you back to the past made it so famous, it had long queues of customers every day ..." '

Kohtake read the opening out loud and read the rest to herself.

'That's an old magazine. It's a surprise someone still has it,' Nagare said while filling a bag with the coffee beans that Mutsuo ordered.

'I found it in a second-hand bookshop. It even includes the rules,' Mutsuo replied with a proud smile.

The magazine stated five rules.

1. When you go back to the past, you can only meet people who have visited the cafe.
2. No matter how hard you try, you cannot change the present.
3. A ghost sits in the chair that takes you back to the past.
4. When you go back to the past, you cannot get up or move from the chair.
5. There is a time limit.

Kohtake held the magazine up. 'In conclusion, it says that it's not clear if you can actually go back in time at this cafe. They should be sued for libel!' She puffed out her cheeks crossly.

'Customer numbers have never changed much,' said Nagare, scratching his head. 'OK, here you are. One bag of coffee beans. One thousand two hundred yen, please.'

Nagare presented Mutsuo with the bagged coffee beans and percussively tapped the keys of the cash register.

'Uh ... yeah,' Mutsuo faltered. 'Thank you for this.' He returned the now-folded towel and paid.

'At any rate, I don't see a problem if your wife wishes to go back in time, but I don't recommend it if she is not on board ... It doesn't matter whether she believes it or not, but in order to return to the past, she will have to follow the rules. The magazine didn't mention it, but if you go back to the past, you must drink an entire cup of coffee before it goes cold. If your wife went back and didn't drink all her coffee, she would become a ghost and end up sitting continually at that table.'

'Wha-what?' Mutsuo looked over at the woman in the white dress.

'For people like your wife in particular, their regrets are strong. The stronger their affection for a lost loved one, or pet, the harder the second parting can be . . . even more so than the first parting. Drinking the coffee might sound simple, but once lost in a flood of emotions, your wife may not notice the coffee getting cold until it is too late.'

Mutsuo was stewing uneasily on Nagare's words, 'the stronger their affection for a lost loved one'. *And I know Sunao thought of Apollo as her child . . .*

'First talk it through properly with your wife,' added Kohtake gently, as if Mutsuo's feelings were painted on his face.

'Yes, of course. Thank you, I'm glad I had this talk.' Mutsuo took the coffee beans, nodded courteously, and turned to leave.

'Before you go,' Nagare called to stop him. 'I think it is still raining outside, so . . .' He brought an umbrella from the back room and handed it to Mutsuo.

'Oh, thank you.'

'No problem.'

After giving several nods of thanks, Mutsuo left the cafe.

CLANG-DONG

'It's a cruel rule, don't you think?' muttered Kohtake after Mutsuo had gone.

'Oh?'

'If people could do things again, there would be no regrets . . . His wife probably never even considered the possibility that her beloved dog would draw his last breath while she was asleep. I can only imagine how awful she must have felt – stuck wondering how and why she fell asleep, knowing he was gone for ever.'

Kohtake was not blaming the cafe's rules.

She was simply wondering how devastated Mutsuo's wife would have felt – not being there for her precious dog's final moments because she fell asleep.

'If only the present could be changed, right?'

'Yes, if only.'

'Why does it have to be that you cannot move from the chair? Even if you must stay in the cafe, it would be good to be able to move about.'

'I have thought the same for a long time.'

'Right? And why does it have to be coffee? Why not tea?'

'Er, no. I actually think coffee is best . . .'

'Yes, I suppose you do,' chuckled Kohtake. 'Well, I'll be off, then. I don't suppose I could borrow an umbrella too?'

'Yes, of course.'

While Kohtake made her way to the cash register and was getting ready to pay, Nagare went to fetch an umbrella from the back room.

Left alone, Kohtake placed coins for the coffee on the coin tray. 'You cannot change the present no matter how hard you try . . . what a cruel rule,' she muttered.

On Nagare's return, she received the umbrella and departed the cafe with a 'Bye, then.'

A few days later, the summer monsoon ended. Weather lore says that thunderstorms mark the end of the summer monsoon, but they are not a clear gauge. The summer monsoon is declared over when the monsoonal cloud systems covering Japan, and the accompanying rainy days, give way to hot sunny days. But there is no clear end to the summer monsoon, and the cloud systems can sometimes creep back and hang around.

Several days after Mutsuo visited the cafe, the summer monsoon was declared over. The temperature soared above thirty degrees Celsius, and the real summer heat began.

Under this cloudless sky, a woman stood outside the cafe with an umbrella in one hand. She was Sunao Hikita, Mutsuo's wife.

Sunao had been pausing for a while, looking at the sign placed at the cafe entrance. *So, this is the place Mutsuo was talking about: the cafe where you can return to the past.*

It had one entrance – through a brick archway. A stairway lit by several wall lamps led down to the basement.

I still don't know what I'm doing here, but here goes . . .

Sunao inhaled determinedly and began slowly to descend the stairs. It was somewhat cooler than under the blazing sun. But with suddenly no breeze, sweat began beading on her forehead. At the bottom of the second flight of stairs, she came to a large wooden door.

Well, if it's true I get to see Apollo again.

Sunao opened the door.

CLANG-DONG

She entered a short passage. In stark contrast to the stiflingly hot air of the stairway, inside was cool.

It's co-cold.

Left bare by a short-sleeved blouse, her arms shivered, probably due to her perspiration. She edged forward tentatively. It was soon apparent the real entrance was halfway down the passage. At the other end of the passage was a door with a sign saying Toilet hanging from it.

Sunao stepped from the passage into the cafe. The room was dimly lit and more cramped than she expected, with three two-seater tables and three stools at the counter. It was more the size of a cosy bar than a cafe.

Then, unexpectedly from behind the counter, a voice softly murmured, 'Hello. Welcome.' It was Kazu Tokita.

What?

This unenergetic customer greeting sounded so strange to Sunao, who had worked part-time at restaurants while at university.

Perhaps strangers are not welcome here?

But her doubt dissipated as she glanced around to see that neither the middle-aged man in the seat closest to her nor the

woman wearing a white dress in the far seat even acknow-
ledged her presence.

'Do you mind sitting at the counter?' Kazu asked, again
with a soft voice.

'Er, no. Actually, I just came to return an umbrella my husband borrowed.'

I wish I hadn't said that. Immediately it felt the wrong reply.
It wasn't a lie to say she came to return the umbrella. But then,
that wasn't her only reason for coming here, either.

To return to the past and meet Apollo one last time.

That was her real reason for coming. Yet, in her heart, she
couldn't believe in returning to the past. The idea that someone could really do such a thing was preposterous. So she
found it hard to mention. And lost in that, she blurted out that
she had an umbrella she came to return.

'Oh . . . OK,' replied Kazu, fully accepting Sunao's words.
She stopped what she was doing and came out from behind
the counter.

'You came just for that? Thank you.' Kazu nodded politely,
took the umbrella and headed to the back room.

'No problem.'

That got her errand out of the way. But she couldn't move
from the spot. Her real purpose for coming was something
else.

*What do I do now? I've just said I only came to return the
umbrella. Perhaps I'll leave and come back another day . . .*

Kazu reappeared. She returned behind the counter and

resumed wrapping paper napkins around fork and spoon pairs.

The waitress is pretending not to look at me, but I'm sure she's wondering why I'm not leaving . . . What should I do? Should I just tell her I want to go back in time? What if she tells me she has no idea what I am talking about? . . . Imagine if she says that – I would be too embarrassed to come here again . . . If only I had read the magazine Mutsuo handed me more carefully . . . I came without telling him too, oh what should I do?

Her perspiration, which had so profusely erupted earlier, had now completely evaporated and she felt colder. She looked up and met eyes with Kazu, who had paused her work and looking her way.

'Was there anything else, perhaps?' Kazu asked.

'Huh?' Sunao feigned nonchalance, but inwardly felt relieved. She was thankful for anything to start a conversation.

'Well, actually, if it's not too much trouble, could I have a glass of water, please?'

'A glass of water?'

'Yes, today's a little hot outside. I'm quite thirsty . . .'

'Yes, of course.'

Kazu poured a glass of water and placed it on the counter.

'Here you go.'

'Thank you.'

Slinking up to the counter, Sunao took the glass. There was no ice, but the water was well chilled. As she swallowed, she smelled the subtle aroma of lemon. It was refreshing and easy to drink.

She hadn't really been thirsty, but she still downed the entire glass.

'Thank you. I'll be off now,' said the man at the table seat closest to the entrance suddenly as he stood up. With a magazine that had been spread out on the table now tucked under his arm, he came to the cash register and presented the order slip. 'How much?'

'Three hundred and eighty yen,' said Kazu as she took the order slip and hammered the keys.

'OK, here we are,' the man said as he plucked a five-hundred-yen coin from the wallet hanging around his neck.

'Receiving five hundred yen.'

As Kazu pushed down the keys, the man stared hard at the woman in the white dress.

'And that's one hundred and twenty yen in change.'

The man took the change from Kazu and stowed it in his wallet, then went out without further comment.

CLANG-DONG

This left just Sunao, Kazu and the woman in the white dress in the room. Sunao must have been a mysterious customer from Kazu's point of view. She claimed to have come only to return an umbrella, but then had hung around just to drink water. Not that she was even a customer, as she hadn't actually ordered anything.

But Kazu said nothing. In fact, even if Sunao hung around like this for hours, Kazu would most likely just continue with her work unperturbed. It was becoming clear to Sunao that Kazu was not one to pry, no matter what the conversation.

'Actually, on second thoughts, could I have an orange juice, please?'

'Certainly,' Kazu replied, with no change in expression whatsoever. This confirmed Sunao's opinion: Kazu was tactful enough not to point out her earlier assertion about only coming to return the umbrella.

In a flash, she had filled in the order slip and disappeared into the kitchen. Watching her go, Sunao made up her mind.

I'll tell her the truth.

Thirteen years ago.

'I got a puppy,' Mutsuo said happily as he peered at the puppy inside the pet carrier. He hadn't even consulted me.

'You didn't even ask me,' I said in a huff to Mutsuo, who shamelessly replied, 'No, I didn't.'

'We can't have a dog in our apartment.'

'My father's house is vacant. We can move there.'

Mutsuo's father's house was a condominium in Jimbocho. He and his father had lived there until we got married. But his father was no longer with us. He had passed away unexpectedly from a heart attack. Mutsuo's mother had divorced and left them when he was little, and he had no siblings. The mortgage on the condominium was paid off, so I had no reason to object to moving.

'Are you really going to keep it?'

'Don't you like dogs?'

'It's not that,' I replied, but truth be told, I didn't. Well, not dogs per se; it was a general feeling I had about pets. They were all a nuisance.

'Do you know how hard it is to take care of a dog? You have to take it for a walk every day, feed it, make sure it stays healthy . . . You do know they don't live very long, right?'

'I'm sure we'll manage,' said Mutsuo, taking out the little puppy from the pet carrier. It was a male golden retriever.

That was how Apollo came into my life. Then, when we began to care for Apollo, I discovered something surprising. I learned that dogs have feelings too.

Don't get me wrong, I never thought they were totally emotionless. But when I started rearing him, I realized he showed emotions no different from ours. In addition to basic happy, cross, sad and excited, he also got depressed when scolded and pleased when praised.

The most surprising of such times was while I was watching a drama, crying. Apollo ambled up to me and peered at my face. I thought, surely not, but I knew his eyes were saying, *Why are you crying? Are you OK? I'm here, you know.*

He didn't need to speak the words for me to know what he was saying. He even licked the tears from my cheek lovingly, as if he understood what they meant. That was the first time I felt someone really *got me*. This communication without words made me realize how eyes spoke to us as much as mouths did.

Apollo was also prone to loneliness and hated to be left by himself in a room. When at his loneliest, I could be just taking out the rubbish and he'd be pleading with me, *Don't leave me!* My heart couldn't help melting when Apollo was like that. It was like I was dealing with an innocent baby.

He was demanding my presence, body and soul, and as Mutsuo and I had no baby of our own I came to love him from my heart. I felt that Apollo had started calling me Mummy. And at some point, I began referring to myself as Mummy, and Mutsuo as Daddy.

After talking it over with Mutsuo, I decided to change my work to something I could do at home. Thanks to the condominium Mutsuo's father left us, even Mutsuo's income alone was enough for us, provided we lived modestly, and Mutsuo readily supported my decision. My new lifestyle came to revolve around Apollo. Then as time went on, Apollo began to understand things beyond the words we uttered. For example, the word no.

People say 'no' to pets to get them to stop what they're doing. But when we said 'no', Apollo could tell whether we were serious or joking. I would even venture as far as to say he was reading our states of mind and our emotions.

We would say the same thing, 'Apollo, no! Stop it,' and if I was serious, especially when I was in a bad mood, he would immediately stop. But if I was having fun, and looking on and laughing at what Apollo was doing, then he would just keep on doing it and never stop.

'Apollo, who's in the wrong, Mummy or Daddy?'

Daddy.

'Shall we give you a bath?'

Those soap bubbles stink.

'Let me sleep just five more minutes.'

No. Wake up. Get up and take me for a walk.

'Come on, we're going out.'

Hurray!

'Goodnight.'

OK, goodnight.

After being with us for ten years, Apollo would hear me say, 'Goodnight,' and immediately curl up and go to sleep. He had started to show his age and easily got tired. Ten years for us are like seventy for dogs. From about that time, Apollo clearly seemed to treat me like a daughter. Out of nowhere, I was no longer the one looking after Apollo; he was looking after me.

I was grateful for Apollo's existence. I think it was because Mutsuo and I had never managed to have a baby all the time we had been married. We had even tried fertility treatment.

Basically, we were yet to be blessed with a baby. It's not that we ever abandoned hope. But I can't help but wonder: if Apollo had never entered my life, how much more sorrowful would it have been?

Perhaps tensions would have arisen between me and Mutsuo, who loved kids. Apollo had been a binding force in our marriage.

Kazu returned from the kitchen and stood in front of Sunao.

'Here you are.'

'Um . . .' Sunao muttered, as Kazu was placing the orange juice down on the counter. If she was going to say something, now was the only opportunity. If she said, 'Thank you,' then she thought the conversation would be over before she could say anything more.

'Yes?' Kazu replied softly, her voice ringing with clarity. Her pupils seemed to suck Sunao in. As Sunao stared into them, she felt weirdly that she could say absolutely anything.

'Well . . . the thing is . . . my husband said . . . that if I came to this cafe, I could return to the past,' said Sunao in a soft voice as if mumbling to herself, leaving intervals of silence.

Kazu listened quietly without interjecting.

'I want to return to the past. That's why I came.'

Sunao then talked about Apollo, about how she regretted falling asleep in his last moments. She explained how her husband recommended that she return to the past and told her the rules.

'But I'm in two minds about it. My husband said that I could return to the past, but I wouldn't be able to leave the cafe. Is that true?'

'Yes. That's right. To be precise, you sit on a chair that takes you back to the past, and you must not move from that chair. That includes standing up. Even hovering above the seat is not permitted,' Kazu said matter-of-factly.

'So that means that even if I can return to the past, I can't do so to care for Apollo in his last moments.'

'That's right. You can't,' Kazu said, making no attempt to cushion her words. She told it as it was.

When Sunao had asked Mutsuo the same question, he had considered the shock she might receive and muddied the waters by saying, 'That might be the case. But perhaps there is something I am unaware of. Who knows, maybe there is a special rule.'

Mutsuo wasn't trying to hide anything. He had just not been able to be frank and say, 'No. You can't,' like Kazu had done. He had to consider how her reaction would impact their relationship as a long-standing married couple. And how it would affect his recommendation that she go back to the past.

Mutsuo may have been blatantly lying when he mentioned a special rule. But he had no ill intentions. Rather, he was simply guided by a very human desire to preserve what morsel of hope Sunao had left.

That lie was necessary for his and Sunao's relationship. Sunao had been saved by this kind of thoughtfulness from Mutsuo on countless occasions before, and she found it accept-able because they were Mutsuo's words. Such thoughtfulness was an important part of their relationship. But she had no such relationship with Kazu. She did not want Kazu to be thinking about such things.

She came to the cafe with the clear intention of learning the facts. If Kazu had answered in the same way as Mutsuo, it would only have clouded her feelings.

'Oh, OK. That's basically all I wanted to know.'

Sunao took her phone from her shoulder bag and opened a photo of Apollo. A seemingly smiling Apollo was being hugged by Sunao and Mutsuo.

'All his life, Apollo gave his everything to live for me and my husband. He gave us so much happiness. So I have no wish to return to the past to try my best to extend Apollo's life. Ever since we started keeping Apollo, I knew his life would be short and the time to say goodbye would come eventually.'

A tear ran down Sunao's cheek.

'But I do regret not being able to nurse Apollo in his last moments. I was never even able to say goodbye . . .'

The ice in her orange juice rattled.

The three large pendulum clocks ticked away the time inside the cafe which did not even have any background music playing.

Sunao could not say the next words. She gripped her phone, sobbing.

Kazu did nothing but stare at the orange juice.

Flap.

Sunao heard the sound of a book closing behind her. She turned around to see the woman in the white dress standing up silently.

Oh, that's right, I wasn't the only customer here.

Sunao wiped her tears, slumped forward and reached for her orange juice.

I guess I'll just drink this and leave. I sort of already knew it, but now I know for sure that I can't return to the past to be with Apollo in his last moments. It's time just to forget the whole thing.

The woman in the white dress passed silently behind Sunao and headed to the toilet.

I may as well leave now.

Sunao left about a third of her orange juice undrunk and got up from her stool.

As she did, Kazu, who was now tidying away the cup at the seat the woman in the white dress had been using, called to her, 'The chair is vacant. Will you be sitting down?'

'What?'

For a moment, Sunao didn't know what Kazu was talking about. Her confusion trapped her in the process of getting off the stool, with just one foot on the floor.

'If you want to go back to the past, you need to sit on this chair.'

'Oh, I don't think I will be going back to the past . . .'

'That's fine. It's completely up to you whether you go back or not.'

That was all Kazu said, and after wiping the table with a cloth, she walked into the kitchen.

Certainly, Kazu hadn't told her to sit there explicitly. She simply asked, 'Will you be sitting down?'

Oh, that's right . . .

Sunao recalled what Mutsuo had told her about the rules.

'A ghost?'

'Yes. According to this magazine, a ghost is always seated on the chair that takes you back to the past.'

'You're kidding, right?'

'No. Well, that's what the article says, anyway. Apparently, you can only ever sit on the chair that takes you to the past while the ghost has gone to the toilet.'

'Oh, OK. But why should I do it? Based on what you just said, if I can't move, what point is there of going back?'

'You would get to see Apollo one more time.'

'I guess so, but . . .'

'I think you should.'

'Why do you think that?'

'If you don't, you might keep living with a feeling of regret. I'm sure Apollo wouldn't want that. You should meet Apollo and let him hear everything you're feeling right now.'

'Isn't that just for our convenience?'

'I think Apollo would want to hear. I think he'd want you to go.'

'That's just your projection.'

'I guess so, but still . . .'

Sunao got up from the stool and stood in front of the chair that the woman in the white dress had been sitting on.

Well, I never got to attend his last moments.

There are many crossroads in life. All regrets stem from

what happened at one moment we never imagined would happen to us. When our own action brings about an unexpected result, how can we not experience huge regret? After all, do we ever get another shot?

I fell asleep. I wanted to be with him at the very end because he could never stand being alone; it made him so sad to be left in a room by himself.

I left Apollo to die alone. I fell asleep and he must have felt so lonely, so sad, while breathing his last, to know I had fallen asleep.

I'm too filled with remorse to rid that thought from my mind. I guess, even if I were to return to the past, all I could do would be to apologize to Apollo.

I can't ask for forgiveness. I don't even feel I have the right to say goodbye. But still . . .

Sunao's heart sank, and her sobbing intensified. The splatter of her tears hitting the floor was audible.

Even so, I want to see Apollo again. I want to see his face. It's selfish of me. I know. But still, I want to see Apollo one more time.

'Will you be sitting down?' asked Kazu behind her.

Sunao turned to Kazu, showing her reddened eyes. 'Yes. Please let me return to a time when Apollo was alive.'

'Very well.'

Once again, Kazu did not ask why Sunao wanted to go back to the past. When Sunao sat down in the chair, Kazu returned from the kitchen carrying a tray with a silver kettle and a white cup.

'You know the rules, right?'

'Yes. Well . . . actually, I'm not sure about the time limit. How long exactly do I have?'

'This is what you need to know . . .' Kazu proceeded to explain the rules while she placed the white coffee cup on a saucer in front of Sunao.

The cup still had nothing inside it.

'I will now pour your coffee. Your experience in the past will only be for the time from when the coffee is poured until it gets cold.'

'Until the coffee gets cold?'

'Yes.'

Sunao pondered this while staring at the empty cup. She had never timed how long it takes for a cup of coffee to go cold.

Ten minutes? Fifteen minutes? No, it's probably not that long.

Sunao's face expressed dismay at the vagueness of the time limit. But Kazu must have been able to read Sunao's look of distress.

'I will also give you this . . .' she said as she picked up what looked like a small stirrer from the tray and placed it in the coffee cup.

'What is that?'

'When placed in the coffee, it sounds an alarm just before the coffee gets cold. As soon as you hear it, please quickly drink all the coffee.'

'So, I just need to drink when the alarm sounds?'

'Yes.'

'OK, got it.' Sunao closed her eyes for a moment.

She noticed her breathing was becoming shallower as her heart rate quickened.

'Are you ready?'

'Um, just one more question.'

'Yes, of course.'

'It's really true that there is nothing I can do to change the present, right?'

'Yes. Nothing will change,' she replied instantly.

It was the reply that Sunao expected.

For example, even if she asked Mutsuo to be with her at that time to prevent her from sleeping, Mutsuo would be unable to take the necessary action to change the present reality that Sunao fell asleep.

She already knew, but she wanted to confirm.

'I understand. Please pour the coffee.'

'Then here we go.'

Kazu lifted the silver kettle, and softly said, 'Before the coffee gets cold.'

With an efficient and graceful movement, she tilted the kettle towards the cup. Coffee poured silently from the narrow spout. It looked like a single black line. Soon, the cup was filled with coffee.

Sunao felt her body begin to ripple and swirl like vapour, but strangely, she was not afraid.

I want to see Apollo.

Sunao's heart was filled with that simple thought. Suddenly she felt lighter, and her entire body was engulfed in a sensation of being sucked up by the heavens above. The scenes she was seeing around her were coming from above and streaming down below. It felt just like her view of the cafe was a video playing in rewind.

My husband and I aren't able to have children. In my seventh year of marriage, I learned from a hospital check-up that I have a body that makes it difficult to conceive. Apollo was five at the time.

Mutsuo wanted children, but having Apollo, he wasn't in a hurry, so we leisurely proceeded with trying to conceive. It was just after that time that it happened. Apollo had got all muddy on a walk in the rain, so I was giving him a bath.

'Come on, Apollo, in you get. In the bath. Apollo, Mummy's calling you.'

'Huh?'

'What's wrong? Why are you looking so surprised?'

'Did you just say Mummy right now?'

'I did. What's wrong? You didn't like it?'

'No, it's not that I didn't like it.'

'Great. I thought I might throw it out there, I was a little scared how you'd react.'

'You had this on your mind all along?'

'Not all along, but I've been waiting for the time to say it for a while.'

'So, you're Daddy?'

'Well, yeah, I guess.'

Looking embarrassed, Mutsuo scratched his head.

'Anyway, thank you.'

'Uh-huh.'

'Really, thank you.'

I had been feeling down after hearing the test results at the hospital.

It is my fault that we haven't had children.

I had always been aware of Mutsuo's love for them. It must have been shocking news that we might never have any.

It was his bad luck to marry me . . .

Mutsuo had saved me from those thoughts. That moment felt like Mutsuo and I had become a real family with Apollo. Yet I had left Apollo to die alone.

I'm sorry, Apollo. I guess you can't forgive your mummy, how could you?

'*Ruff!*'

I awoke to the nostalgia of hearing Apollo's bark.

As I opened my eyes, I saw that the person behind the counter was not the waitress who had just poured my coffee but a large man wearing a cook's uniform, standing there like a demon statue guarding a temple. I had heard Apollo, but he didn't seem to be anywhere.

'*Ruff. Ruff. Ruff!*'

'Apollo! No. Shush.'

I could hear Apollo and Mutsuo outside. The man in the

uniform came from behind the counter, and after nodding politely to me, he stamped loudly over to the entrance.

'Apollo. Bad boy. Settle down. Be quiet.'

'Oh, it's OK.'

'I'm really sorry about this.'

'*Ruff. Ruff.*'

'How odd, he doesn't normally bark like this.'

'*Ruff!*'

Mutsuo and Apollo were yet to appear. Simply based on Apollo's bark, I could tell it was about one year earlier. It was when his joints had weakened, but he would still come on walks. Mutsuo had told me that he sometimes dropped into the cafe to buy coffee beans while on a walk with Apollo.

'Apollo . . .' I thought it was going to be a loud yell, but my voice was soft and thin, as if I was talking to myself.

'*Ruff.*'

Even so, Apollo barked from behind the wall as if in response to my cry.

'Apollo!'

That had made me more joyful, and this time I called his name loudly.

'Who is that? Is that Mummy?' I could hear Mutsuo say.

'*Ruff. Ruff. Ruff!*'

Dragged inside by barking Apollo, Mutsuo appeared at the entrance.

'Apollo. Wait. No!' Mutsuo held Apollo back from running over. Apollo was twelve years old. He no longer leaped and bounded in excitement, but he was still wagging his tail vigorously as he pulled Mutsuo along.

'Oh, don't worry. That lady over there is our only customer right now,' the man in the cook's uniform said from behind Mutsuo, and he gave me a questioning glance.

You've come from the future to meet someone, right?

I nodded a little.

'Oh, I'm very sorry.'

Mutsuo bowed his head as he was pulled along by Apollo. They came right up in front of me.

'Ruff.'

Once Apollo had reached me, he sat, and while panting with his tongue out, he put his head forward. It was what he did when he wanted a pat.

With my trembling hand, I gently stroked his head. I felt Apollo's warmth through my palm.

It was not Apollo lying cold after drawing his last breath. He was alive. I had never imagined that I could once again feel his warmth. Apollo seemed satisfied from my patting and lay down at my feet.

He looked quite exhausted from pulling Mutsuo around. While my attention had been focused on Apollo, Mutsuo had sat down in the chair on the other side of the table.

'What's going on? Why are you here?' Mutsuo was looking at me intently.

'You must be surprised.'

'Of course I am. I thought you said you couldn't join us because you were visiting your parents.'

'Oh, that me?'

'What?'

'Er, never mind . . . What are you saying?'

'I'm not following you. But whatever. Er . . . hold this for a sec, would you?'

Mutsuo handed me Apollo's lead, got up from his chair and walked over to the man in the cook's uniform. After they exchanged glances, Mutsuo dropped his head as if chastising himself.

'So, what's the story?' asked Mutsuo, who had returned to his seat and was now looking down at Apollo.

'What do you mean?'

'What did you come back for?'

'Huh?'

'Oh, come on, I know you're from the future.'

Mutsuo was stealing my time with Apollo, so although he asked an important question, I felt the conversation was pointless.

'Er . . . well, yes.'

Mutsuo had that side to him. He would feign ignorance when he knew something, and tiptoe around the subject.

Even the time when I learned that I was the reason why I couldn't get pregnant, he had dissipated the tension by saying, 'OK. No problem,' as if he was replying to me telling him, 'Sorry, there's only curry for dinner tonight.'

The time when he first referred to me as Mummy was another example of that. Although he had thought about it – as in really thought it through – his delivery embodied pure sprezzatura.

Now was no exception, he pretended to be confused, which made it easier for a conversation to flow. The more I think about it, the more examples of him helping me out that way come to mind.

He was helping me out again at this moment. I wasn't sure if I should talk about coming from the future or not. And perhaps he had already gathered the reason I came. Therefore, all I needed to say was, 'Apollo . . .'

Nothing else needed to be said; Mutsuo understood everything. 'Oh, I see,' he said sadly, looking at Apollo.

During this time, it was taboo for us to talk about Apollo's age, to mention how many years he might have left.

Just the thought brought on tears.

'Did he suffer at the end?'

As soon as he asked, my heart felt squeezed like it would burst. After all, how could I, who had fallen asleep, answer that question. Tears began to flow. I felt apologetic and ashamed. I was filled with regret. I felt I had let Mutsuo down too.

But I couldn't lie. At least with Mutsuo, I should speak honestly. Even if he didn't know now, he would find out eventually.

'Well, the thing is . . . I couldn't manage to be there for Apollo in his final moments.'

Whatever happens, no matter how much I regret it, that past is unchangeable.

'Mutsuo, you had work, so you weren't there that day. It was just me. I was giving Apollo water with a syringe and taking just a little food myself.'

74

My voice was wavering. It was the first time I had ever spoken in detail about what happened that day. To Mutsuo in the future, I had only said, 'He died because I fell asleep.'

Mutsuo had said lots of words to console me, but I mostly don't remember what he said.

'I had set up a spacious sleeping area so that I could always be by Apollo's side.'

'I see.'

'We worked together to ensure one of us was always awake.'

'OK.'

Mutsuo sat there listening quietly, throwing in the appropriate replies.

'But despite it all, on that day, after Apollo had willingly taken water for the first time in a while, he opened his eyes and smiled at me, also for the first time in what seemed like ages. I lay down with him to give him a hug, and I felt happy feeling Apollo's warm body and breathing.'

'Go on.'

'He's still alive; he's still OK. As I was thinking that, lying there, I was intending to get up, but I fell into a dream.

'Two hours had gone before I realized, lying right next to him . . .'

I involuntarily closed my eyes hard.

I couldn't put it into words.

Tears ran down my cheeks and fell from my jaw.

'I'm sorry, Mutsuo. For no fault of your own, I've been taking it out on you.'

'A-ha-ha! You mean me in the future?'

'Oh, I guess so.'

'You seem to have suffered a fair bit.'

'Yeah.'

'But you need to let it go. You've done nothing wrong, Sunao. Apollo was clearly happy. Think about it. You were hugging him right to the end. Isn't that right? Apollo?'

'*Ruff!*'

'See, Apollo says he agrees with me.'

My tears didn't stop. Mutsuo's words had saved me again. Apollo rubbed his head against me. He did that when he wanted praise or when he was happy. I hugged him with all my might.

I kissed him, and I patted him all over, stretching my hand as far as I could while sitting down. That was when I heard it.

Beep, beep, beep, beep, beep . . .

An alarm sounded.

I had completely forgotten. I needed to drink the coffee before it went cold. Even Mutsuo, who had not known about the alarm, caught on to what it was for.

'Time's up?'

'Yes.'

'Well, drink up then.'

'OK.'

With Mutsuo telling me what to do, I drank all the coffee. The past was unchanged; I had still fallen asleep. Even so, I was glad that I had come back. I met Mutsuo in the past, and I was able to see Apollo once again.

While thinking that thought, my body began to go all billowy as it had done when I came here. My hands were still patting Apollo's head.

'Did you know?' said Mutsuo suddenly as he extended his hand over mine, while I was patting Apollo's head.

'What?'

'Apollo always waits for you to go to bed before he sleeps.'

'What?'

For a moment, I didn't understand what Mutsuo was saying.

'Wait a sec, what do you mean?'

'How could you know, right? You are always asleep already.'

'I always waited for Apollo to sleep.'

Then I went to sleep. When I said, 'Goodnight,' Apollo would immediately get in his bed and start breathing like he was asleep.

After I saw that Apollo was sleeping, I went to bed. We did that every day.

'You're wrong about that.'

'How am I wrong?'

'After you go to bed, Apollo always gets up and checks that you are asleep before he goes to sleep.'

'Really?'

'Once you are sleeping, Apollo goes to bed himself.'

'You're joking?'

'You have stayed up at night alone crying before, right?'

'Er . . .'

I remembered back to my thirty-third birthday. The second in vitro fertilization procedure failed, and I decided to give up

77

on treatment. We had Apollo, after all. But even so, when I thought about it, there had been nights when I was up alone, sad for some reason.

I remembered how on those nights, Apollo would stay by my side.

'Maybe because of those nights, Apollo pretends to sleep and then waits for you to go to sleep. Then, after making sure you are asleep, he always licks your eyes, and then goes back to bed.'

'Surely not.'

'So, I don't think it's true to say you abandoned his death bed.'

'Wait . . .'

'Apollo was just waiting for you to fall asleep.'

'I . . .'

'Apollo probably checked that you were properly sleeping and then, relieved, fell asleep.'

I don't really recall much after that. I began sobbing profusely, I hugged Apollo with all my might and said thank you continuously until my voice was hoarse. But what I do faintly remember was Apollo lovingly licking my cheeks while barking, '*Ruff. Ruff.*'

'Move!'

When she returned to her senses, Mutsuo and Apollo were gone, and the scary-faced woman in the white dress was standing in front of Sunao.

'Oh! I'm sorry.' Sunao got up out of the chair in a hurry, gesturing to the woman in the white dress to take it. She walked slowly and clumsily, probably on account of her tear-soaked eyes.

'How did it go?'

The sudden question came from behind her. It was Kazu.

Sunao looked around, still in disbelief she had returned to the present.

Apollo?

Kazu cleared away the cup Sunao had used and disappeared into the kitchen. The woman in the white dress read her book quietly as if nothing had happened.

Now all that entered Sunao's eyes were the three large pendulum clocks ticking away at different times, the rotating wooden ceiling fan and the woman in the white dress. In this room with no windows, the passing of time was impossible to fathom.

Gosh, was it all a dream?

She felt no sign of Apollo, who just moments earlier was by her side.

But Apollo certainly had been here. The warmth of Apollo, who she knew was dead, still lingered in her hand and in her cheeks.

Soon, Kazu returned carrying a coffee for the woman in the white dress.

'What has just happened?'

'By that, you mean?'

'The present does not change, right?'

'That's right.'

'The past doesn't change, either?'

'No, it doesn't.'

'Then why do I feel like I have returned a completely different person?' Sunao asked Kazu with imploring eyes.

However, with a nonchalant expression, Kazu replied, 'Well, that I don't know.'

'Oh, OK then.'

Sunao, still teeming with feelings, settled her bill and left the cafe. The sun had begun to set, and the town was painted orange. The shadows stretched out long.

I was deep in thought as I walked home.

What just happened to me?

I have been engulfed with regret over the past. It had consumed me; there was nowhere I could purge it from me, and there had been nothing that could save me. Yet now, I am inundated by quite a weird feeling. If I were to give it a name, then I guess it must be . . .

gratitude.

No other word seems to match. Now, all I want is to go home and tell Mutsuo.

I am sure he'll laugh and say, 'You're telling me what I told you in the past?'

I'll let him have his laugh. And I want to tell it all to Apollo too. I haven't been saying anything to him but 'Sorry.' But I'm sure Apollo never wanted to hear that.

He wouldn't have wanted me to cry. So, I'm going to live my life feeling good about myself. That's what I want to say to those two when I get home:

Thank you . . .

III

The Proposal

A proposal was definitely imminent.

Hikari Ishimori began to feel a foreboding as soon as he asked her to meet him at this cafe.

Surely he doesn't intend to propose to me here?

The place was such a dive, she began to doubt his judgement. With only a few lamps hanging from the ceiling, the windowless second-basement room was unpleasantly dim.

What?

Catching her eye were three large pendulum clocks stretching from the floor to the ceiling, each showing a completely different time. After checking her watch, she worked out that only the middle clock was right.

I'm never coming here again.

Those were Hikari's first impressions on visiting this cafe.

He chose the absolute worst timing and location for a proposal.

Hikari gave a huge mental sigh.

She had met Yoji Sakita at a clue-solving gathering. It was the kind of escape-room game in which a number of puzzles had to be solved within a limited time in order to escape. This event had mandated teams of six, so Hikari and two of her girl friends formed a team with a trio of guys Yoji was part of.

Yoji liked clue-solving games and Hikari later heard that at the weekend he liked to go to such events even alone.

Nerd with glasses. That was her first impression of Yoji. She was sure he would have been called a nerd in elementary school.

With this image in her mind, Hikari held back her laughter each time Yoji did his signature quirk of pushing his glasses up his nose.

Through that game event, the six of them became friends and started to hang out frequently.

Six months later, Hikari was still under the impression that this group relationship was continuing as before, but to her dismay, she found out two couples had formed in the group.

That left just two: Hikari and Yoji. Egged on by the other four, they too started going out. The time Yoji proposed to her at this cafe was the third Christmas Eve since they met.

'I'd like us to wait a little longer before we discuss marriage.'

Hikari delivered her words just as Yoji took out the ring box. They had been going steady for one year. Every now and then, there had been tell-tale signs that marriage was on Yoji's mind, and that a day like this would come.

'Don't get me wrong. It's not that I don't want to get married.'

Her honest thought was, *I'm not sure you're the one.*

But she was afraid to communicate that and risk hurting his feelings. He was the perfect boyfriend. Hikari's enthusiasm for the clue-solving games that had brought them together was probably now even greater than his. And he was a civil servant, which meant a secure income.

Even so, the sheer thought of marriage brought on heavy feelings of reluctance. But it wasn't the future so much that unnerved her.

What if a marriage candidate more suitable than Yoji appears?

Such lingering vague expectancy was denying her the confidence that she wouldn't regret marrying him. She was still twenty-eight years old. If she skipped this marriage, there would be a next time.

She had female friends who had married around twenty-four or twenty-five, but who now were divorcing, one after the other.

Perhaps it was marriage itself she was uncertain about. As long as she lived alone, she at least had no inconveniences. And she was not brimming with desire to get married.

What's so wrong with how we are now?

She was also aware that whenever Yoji had mentioned marriage, her heart seemed to cool subtly. It wasn't that she didn't like him. It was more a timing thing. Right now, she simply wasn't ready.

Right now . . .

'My work has finally got interesting . . .'

It wasn't a lie. Hikari had changed jobs a year ago to begin working as a bridal planner.

Before the switch, she had a job at a major firm, but she resigned because of her supervisor's toxic behaviour. At her new job, working hours were more irregular than before, a weekend off was a rare occurrence, and her pay was lower too. But she liked her boss, and the work was rewarding.

Even though it was her work, there were many times when she would feel her eyes well up while watching the happy bride and groom in front of her. That was precisely why she thought as she did.

I'm not confident I would be that happy marrying Yoji.

She couldn't take the leap, and she found no words to express that feeling. While aware of how inflexible and annoying she must seem, she didn't want the niggling regret that marriage threatened to cause her.

'I'm sorry I'm being so selfish.'

Hikari said nothing else and dropped her gaze. The coffee in her cup was completely cold, yet its level had not even dropped a millimetre.

'Oh . . . I see. I guess I jumped the gun.'

She looked up to see Yoji's wry smile that followed those words and felt a painful jab in her heart. Her selfishness was causing sorrow. But she couldn't lie to herself.

If she had, and got married, she didn't think it would have brought Yoji happiness.

'I'll be waiting. I'll hang around until your feelings change,' said Yoji, and he drank the entire cup of cold coffee.

'That was last year,' said Hikari to conclude her account of her meeting with Yoji at this cafe.

She had tried to tell it as truthfully as she could remember and described how she felt at the time.

The audience for Hikari's tale were Nagare Tokita, the cafe owner, Kazu Tokita, the waitress, and Fumiko Kiyokawa, a cafe regular who was sitting on a counter stool.

Also present was a woman, quietly reading a book in the furthest seat of the room. She was wearing a short-sleeved white dress and showed no sign of being cold despite it being December. Hikari's story didn't seem to pique her interest, as she never once lifted her eyes from her book.

'What? So, how did it end up with him?' asked Fumiko, who in contrast with the woman in the white dress had been listening to every word.

'He dumped me. Six months ago.'

'He dumped you after promising to wait?'

'Yes.'

'What was his reason?'

'He said he liked someone else . . .'

'What the hell?'

Fumiko threw herself back with a look of disdain.

'Just forget him. What kind of man won't wait half a year? Leave him be and get on with your life. It sounds like you were correct in not marrying him! If he did that, there's no need to return to the past!'

'What?'

Hikari was taken aback. She had only just met Fumiko – and only because they both happened to be in this cafe – yet Fumiko had just gone ahead and drawn her own prejudiced conclusion.

Someone help me out here? Hikari looked pleadingly to Nagare and Kazu behind the counter, but Nagare just folded his arms and vocalized a 'Hmm,' as he furrowed his brow contemplatively.

Kazu's expression remained so blasé as she polished a glass it was hard to tell if she had even been listening.

Who are these people?

She didn't actually believe it was possible to return to the past. Her thoughts were more a desperate grasp at a straw, wishing if only she could go back. Certainly, neither Nagare nor Kazu had told her, 'Unless you provide a good reason, we won't let you go back.'

The question, 'What happened?' was asked by Fumiko. What business it was of Fumiko's to ask such a question was unknown to Hikari, as they had just met. She thought that perhaps Fumiko had been speaking for the other two. That misunderstanding had led her to conclude falsely that she was required to state a reason in order to be allowed to return to the past.

So, she realized that it was wrong of her to be annoyed with those two for not saying anything to her. But nevertheless, she felt embarrassed.

She had no one to blame but herself that she blabbed her story, got annoyed, and then ended up feeling sorry for herself.

What on earth am I doing here?

Just when Hikari was beginning to regret that she had come to this cafe . . .

'You can go back,' came a voice, sounding as one would sound talking to oneself. Hikari looked up to see Kazu, behind the counter. She had paused from her task and was looking back at her.

'Really?'

'Yes.'

Hikari realized that apart from Kazu's greeting, 'Hello. Welcome,' and Nagare's 'Hmm,' Fumiko had been doing all the talking.

She lunged forward towards Kazu as if pouncing on her. It was finally time to get to the point.

'Then let me go back. I want to return to that day, a year ago. Please!'

'Even though going back will be futile?'

Fumiko had again interjected. But this time Hikari was in no mood to be dissuaded.

'How can you say it will be futile? Surely, there's no way of telling until I go back and do things again?'

Fumiko's eyes widened in reaction to the words Hikari had shot at her so emotionally. She immediately responded, 'Sorry,

I didn't explain myself very well.' She looked genuinely apologetic.

On seeing Fumiko's reaction, Hikari regretted her over-heated reply. But Fumiko did not retract what she had said.

'I'm guessing you don't know, do you? . . . You can return to the past. That you can do, but even if you do, no matter how hard you try, you won't be able to change the present.'

'What?'

Fumiko's explanation was not the answer Hikari wanted. That was because she wanted to return to the past to change the present. If not to change the present, then what purpose would there be to return to the past?

'I'm sorry, what are you saying?'

'I'm saying that even if you return to the past and accept his proposal, or even if you propose to him, that will not change the present in which he fell for another woman and left you.'

'But, I mean, why won't the present change?' asked Hikari, with an increasingly unsettled voice.

'Because that is the rule,' replied Kazu matter-of-factly.

'The rule?'

'That's right. You can return to the past, but there are several rules that you must obey.'

Kazu spoke quietly, but the *must* part left no wiggle room. Judging by Kazu's chilly stare, Hikari felt that even if she pushed back, it would be like pushing against a wall.

She had the feeling that any such desperate floundering would be futile. Even so, she was not convinced and tried to push back.

'But what if I promise to marry him?'

'Oh, you can do that.'

'Then . . .'

'But you won't be able to get married.'

The brief glimpse of happiness made Hikari more determined.

'We'll just secure a wedding hall. What could stop us?'

'Even if you booked a venue, the ceremony would be cancelled on the day for some reason. If you tried to register your marriage, it would definitely be impossible to submit it to the registry office.'

Hikari's mind was in turmoil.

If the past changes, the present will also change.

She thought that was universally recognized. Now that had been overturned.

'You're kidding, right?'

Say you're kidding.

'We are completely serious.'

'Why would there be such a rule?'

'Even we don't know the answer to that. But the rule is absolute. Because this rule exists, there is no way you will be able to marry him. Also, he is definitely going to announce his split from you because he has met someone else. During that time, your relationship with him will neither develop nor deteriorate . . . even if you tried to end the relationship before he broke up with you, you would not be able to.'

'Seriously?'

Hikari dropped limply into a seat at the middle table.

I had no idea there would be such an annoying rule.

She had learned that she could go back in time in the cafe in an email from Yoji that she received one day without warning, a few months after the break-up.

About that cafe where I proposed to you.

There's a rumour that you can go back in time there.

No greetings. Hikari shuddered at the two-line email. *Weirdo.* He was the one who broke up with her, and now for some incomprehensible reason he was sending her a cryptic email. It wasn't normal.

Hikari simply ignored it, without even replying. A few days later, she received notice of Yoji's death. That uncanny chain of events left her spooked. She could still remember that strange discomfort. It felt like a revelatory flash of insight when she was playing a clue-solving game – the feeling she got when several unrelated clues threaded together to lead to one answer.

Proposal.

Betrayal.

And not to forget . . . his final email.

Sudden death notice.

Trusting in her intuitive response to those clues, she visited the cafe. If she could go back to the past, she concluded, then surely she could change this present. But that hope was dashed.

'You seem to have taken quite a shock from hearing you can't change the present,' remarked Fumiko as she observed Hikari looking despondently at the ceiling.

'It's a normal response,' commented Nagare.

'Oh, sure.' Fumiko had first-hand experience: she had travelled back in time herself, to meet her boyfriend who had departed for America. At the time, Fumiko didn't know any of the cafe's rules either.

There were five basic rules.

1. While back in time, you can only meet people who have visited the cafe.
2. No matter how hard you try while back in time, you cannot change the present.
3. There is a customer occupying the chair that takes you through time.
4. You cannot move from the chair.
5. There is a time limit.

When she'd learned that you cannot change the present, Fumiko's reaction had been just the same as Hikari's. Nevertheless, she had chosen to go back regardless, if only to vent a complaint or two to her boyfriend who had skipped off to the States. As a result, she couldn't prevent him from going, but she did return knowing his true feelings.

'Oh, by the way, how is your boyfriend in America?' Nagare asked Fumiko seated at the counter.

There was a slight pause when Fumiko, rather than answer, drained the final liquid from her mostly empty coffee cup. 'Oh, er, I'm sure he's fine,' she commented indifferently.

'Haven't you heard from him?'

Fumiko traced her index finger around the rim of the cup on the counter. Based on her behaviour, it was clear even to Hikari, a bystander, that communication with her boyfriend in America was probably non-existent.

'Well, no news is good news.'

Nagare quietly picked up Fumiko's cup and took it to the kitchen to pour a refill.

'I guess so.' With Nagare gone, Fumiko was left muttering to herself.

I don't like her.

Hikari was noticing that she found Fumiko irritating for some reason.

But her annoyance did not stem from the know-it-all manner in which Fumiko – whom she had never met before and who was not even cafe staff – had told her that the present wouldn't change even if she went back in time.

Rather, Hikari could tell, even from the fragments of information she had heard, that the only reason Fumiko had not heard from her boyfriend was because she was too stubborn to contact him.

She's suddenly less talkative now the conversation has turned to her boyfriend.

Sometimes, even without someone saying very much, you can read their emotions from their facial expressions and gestures. She could tell that Fumiko was hiding her true feelings because she was casting her eyes downwards and biting her bottom lip.

No doubt she was frustrated that she hadn't heard from her boyfriend but found herself unable to tell him that.

Who does she think she is?

She was a trim and pretty woman. Her beautifully chiselled face exuded a strong competitive spirit and a high sense of pride. It was obvious to Hikari that such a woman would not think of contacting her man until he contacted her first.

What a fool.

A simple message would have solved it. She had a perfectly contactable partner, and she was choosing to be stubborn for no good reason. Hikari realized she was jealous of Fumiko. The irritation she felt was caused by jealousy.

This woman is beautiful, and she has a boyfriend. She has all the things I don't.

No man would be upset to be told by Fumiko that she liked him. Hikari was jealous of such looks. If Fumiko broke up with her boyfriend in the States, she would soon be dating a different man. There was no way that men would leave her alone. There are few women who can afford to sulk about not getting contacted.

How can God be so unfair. He didn't bestow on me such an advantage. But, regardless, I put off answering Yoji's proposal. As we were the only two remaining in the clue-solving group, I was caught in the flow of the moment, and it just swept me along. But I made the mistake of thinking Yoji liked me not for my looks, but for what was inside. I assumed wrong. I was forgetting that in the end men choose by what they see.

'I'll be waiting.'

Hikari believed those words Yoji had told her. Or she had believed them, until he told her, 'I met someone else,' and she was left feeling like she had got a raw deal.

No, it was probably my fault for making him wait. But even so, I can't help feeling that if I was prettier . . .

She had such an ordinary face with no prominent features. Just fat eyelids, a low nose and thin lips – unlike the elegantly beautiful Fumiko.

If only I had just Fumiko's eyes, or just her nose, or just her lips, maybe Yoji would not have been tempted to get a new girlfriend.

Every feature Hikari desired was arranged perfectly on Fumiko. Hence the source of annoyance.

My ugly jealousy.

She knew what it was. And nothing was really comparable. Yet whenever Yoji's face appeared in her mind, telling her he had met someone else, it felt unbearable.

What would have happened if I had accepted his proposal that day? One thing for sure is that I wouldn't be so repulsively jealous.

But it was too late now. She would never be able to see Yoji again.

'Actually . . .'

Hikari had looked up and was speaking to Fumiko, who had received a second cup of coffee from Nagare. Fumiko was focused on the coffee and didn't immediately catch on that Hikari was talking to her.

'Oh, sorry. Are you talking to me?'

Fumiko returned the cup to its saucer and swivelled round to face Hikari.

'My boyfriend . . .'

'Hmm?'

'He died. After we broke up . . .

'What?'

Fumiko's eyes widened on hearing Hikari's sudden revelation. She exchanged glances with Nagare standing behind the counter.

'He had a pre-existing heart condition. I knew that he sometimes went to the hospital about it.'

While gazing absently at the sugar pot placed on the table, Hikari continued her story as if talking to herself.

'When he broke up with me, I never, ever thought he would die. I remember feeling annoyed at the thought that he must have been put off by my stalling on getting married.'

But . . .

In her heart there was a twinge of doubt.

What if he knew he was terminally ill and concocted a lie about meeting someone else in order to break up with me?

Hikari spontaneously snorted at the thought.

He'd never do that . . .

The idea seemed too neat a solution. She felt embarrassed even to think it.

But what if that was what happened?

The emotions that had kept her in turmoil for the last six months since the break-up would have been misplaced.

How am I meant to react to that?

Noticing Nagare and Fumiko watching her, Hikari gave a little shake of her head.

I can't do anything about it now. Nothing would change. And if the present can't be changed, going back to the past would be useless.

Hikari didn't dare to put into words what was bothering her.

'I thought if I could go back in time, I could at least help by telling him to get treatment before it was too late . . . that maybe if I helped him, we wouldn't have to break up,' she said weakly.

She was accepting that it was impossible to bring back time that had passed. If such a thing was possible, this cafe would be more famous than it was. No doubt it would be packed with customers looking to redress past wrongs. But looking around the dimly lit, windowless room, the only customers were a woman in a white dress and Fumiko.

A cup of coffee on the menu was a mere three hundred and eighty yen.

The most expensive item on the menu was chicken and cream pasta with perilla mint at nine hundred and eighty yen.

It was obvious even to Hikari, who knew nothing about how to run a cafe, that for this number of customers, this menu and pricing couldn't be viable.

If it were possible to go back in time and change the present, customers would come here even if a cup of coffee was ten thousand yen, or even ten times that.

It was therefore clear.

If you cannot change the present by going back in time, this cafe has no value.

98

Hikari was now believing exactly that.

If she could return to the past and save Yoji; if she could accept Yoji's proposal; and if they could live happily together, Hikari would gladly pay a million yen. No, even if the price was ten million yen, she would pay it. If ten million yen could save a person from death, that would still be a bargain.

And yet, this cafe seemed all so drab now she knew the present couldn't be changed. She finally understood. Ordinarily a person would not want to go back in time in this cafe.

'At any rate, I think this was a waste of time. I'm leaving. How much do I owe?'

Hikari stood up and took her coat draped over the chair. She looked at the cash register to see Kazu already waiting there.

After Hikari handed the order slip to Kazu, Kazu replied, 'Three hundred and eighty yen.'

So nondescript. Ever since entering the cafe, Hikari had considered Kazu to be a waitress who strangely lacked presence. Barely speaking a word, she was hardly suited to the service industry. Even when Hikari was talking, it was Fumiko and Nagare who put in the appropriate responses, while Kazu just silently tended to the glasses. She had a wall-like standoffishness.

Although Fumiko's looks made Hikari jealous, she had made a favourable impression because she had listened to her story. As for Nagare, he just responded with grunts while standing with arms folded, but Hikari could tell he was listening intently.

Except for that other customer – the woman in the white dress – it was only Kazu who had seemed detached.

'Are you sure you want to leave like that?' asked that same Kazu to Hikari standing in front of the cash register ready to pay. Hikari didn't immediately understand what she meant. She thought perhaps she had left something behind. She grabbed her shoulder bag and even scanned the seat she had sat in, but she saw nothing.

However . . .

I haven't left anything behind . . . but something seems unresolved.

. . . something was still gnawing at Hikari's chest. But the idea that Kazu was pointing that out seemed impossible. Especially considering that feeling was something Hikari was trying to blank from her own mind.

'Yes,' she reflexively replied while receiving her change from Kazu.

Is it really OK if I leave like this?

To give that answer was a struggle that left Hikari feeling lost. Kazu wasn't keeping her from leaving. She had simply asked, *Are you sure you want to leave like that?* But it had caused the gnawing at her heart to intensify. Before Yoji died, he met her to break up, telling her that he had met someone else. But had he really met another woman? It didn't gel with his earlier promise to wait.

What if he lied about there being another woman in order to break up with me?

If that was so, the story would change. It would mean that

Yoji had intentionally caused those feelings (the anger) that engulfed Hikari when they parted.

Did Yoji plan the break-up deliberately to try to make me hate him?

Why?

Well, I guess it is understandable.

He didn't want me to grieve.

Hold on.

This is all speculation. I'm looking back with rose-tinted glasses.

But still . . . What if Yoji actually did lie to spare me from despair?

Kazu's simple question was setting loose a bundle of emotions she had probably tucked away so as not to think about or notice them. But given Yoji's personality, things were starting to make better sense.

He wasn't the kind of man whose heart would so easily change after saying that he would wait. She wouldn't have liked him as much if he were that man.

What should I do?

Hikari didn't leave after paying, and Fumiko peered at her strangely. Rather than moving from the cash register, Kazu was standing there averting her eyes. If she was an ordinary waitress, then after the payment was finished, she would have bowed her head and said, 'Thank you for coming.' But she hadn't.

Instead, Kazu just seemed to be waiting for something. While Hikari watched Kazu behave this way, something suddenly occurred to her.

'Er, there's one more thing I would like to reconfirm.'

'Sure, what is it?' replied Kazu as if she had been waiting for Hikari's question.

'No matter how hard you try while back in the past . . . that means no matter what you say, you cannot change the present, right?'

'That's right.'

'Even if I tell him he's going to die?'

'Yes.'

'But wouldn't that have an effect on the rest of his life?'

'Even if he is told he will die, there will be no change to the rest of his life. Because that will be protected by the rule that the present does not change.'

'But what about the fact that he knows? What happens to his memory?'

'That will be intact.'

'Completely intact?'

'Well, depending on his personality, he may or may not believe it.'

'So, you mean it is up to him whether he sees it as a joke or takes it seriously?'

'Exactly.'

'I see.'

It was as she had deduced, which therefore meant that she in the present day knew that Yoji liked another woman but Yoji in the past would not know that. Also, whether she chose to go back to the past or not, it would not change the fact he would leave her. But even if the present stayed the same either way, how different would those scenarios be in Yoji's shoes?

What if Yoji, knowing he would die, had lied for my benefit?

Hikari wondered whether perhaps for Yoji, the way he dealt with his impending death would have been completely different if she had accepted his proposal on that day instead of postponing her reply. Although the present would stay unchangeable, she couldn't help feeling his experience might change just a little.

At the very least, the months between that day and the day of his death would be different. Even if he did still meet someone else, that might be all fine and well, and if the other woman was a lie, then so much the better.

Even if this turned out to be pointless for me, it might still be meaningful for Yoji.

Hikari looked up at Kazu, who was still staring at her.

'On second thoughts, I think I will go back. I don't like how things have turned out, so I want to at least try for a slight change.'

'Very well,' Kazu replied curtly. She spun on her heel and walked into the kitchen.

It seemed somewhat anti-climactic not to be asked what made her change her mind after seeming adamant to leave. It felt uncomfortably weird, actually – as if Kazu could read her thoughts.

'What's with the sudden change of mind?' asked Fumiko as Hikari returned to the table. Hikari *had* expected Fumiko to ask, based on what little she knew of her. This time, however, she didn't feel so obliged to tell all.

'I want no regrets,' Hikari simply said.

'Oh, that makes sense,' said Fumiko, and as if stuck in thought, she said nothing else and promptly left the cafe, saying she just remembered there was something she had to do.

The doorbell rang out its CLANG-DONG chime.

Perhaps she had gone to contact her boyfriend in America, or maybe it was something else.

When Hikari said, 'I want no regrets,' she was also insinuating to Fumiko that perhaps being stubborn would lead to regrets. Maybe that message got through. It is up to each individual to decide how they feel about the words of others and what action they wish to take.

Moments earlier, that had been Hikari's decision. She had been on the verge of leaving the cafe when a single casual remark from Kazu changed her mind about wanting to return to the past. Now she thought it might make sense to go back in time, even if the present wouldn't change.

I'll do it for Yoji.

She felt her heart get squeezed tightly by just a vague recollection of how she used to feel when going out with Yoji. Up until now, she had been avoiding even acknowledging such feelings.

So much has happened, this is the first time I'm addressing my feelings level-headedly . . . now that I am . . . I guess I really loved him.

And . . . *There's something I have to make sure of . . .* Hikari was no longer hesitant about going back. She draped her coat over the back of the chair and sat down once again. After a while, Kazu returned from the kitchen.

After pouring Hikari another coffee, Kazu proceeded to inform her of the several other rules, aside from the one about not being able to change the present. She learned that she could only meet people who have visited the cafe; that she must sit in a certain chair in order to go back to the past; and that she could not move from that chair while back in the past.

Hikari considered those rules to be annoying, but none posed a significant hurdle. Just one, however, stuck out as particularly surprising.

'A ghost?'

Kazu had just explained that the woman in the white dress occupying the far seat was in fact a ghost.

Initially, she assumed it must be a joke. But then Kazu continued, 'Yes. In order to go back to the past, you will have to wait until she gets up to go to the toilet.' The sight of Kazu explaining this without changing expression left Hikari speechless. Kazu did not come across as the type to joke.

As they were already talking of going back in time, things could not become stranger – even if a ghost was involved. Therefore, she decided to accept the existence of ghosts. But . . .

'Toilet? She still visits the toilet even though she's a ghost?'

No matter how long she pondered the idea, she couldn't get her head around why a ghost would do that. She stared into Kazu's straight face, still open to the possibility that she would say, 'Just kidding,' but she continued matter-of-factly:

'Yes. Every day, she will go to the toilet just once. It's that window of opportunity when you can sit down.'

Kazu seemed unfazed by any of Hikari's responses of surprise, doubt or shock. She explained that no one knew when the woman in the dress would go to the toilet and that Hikari could stay in the cafe after closing time if she wanted to wait for the chair to be vacant. Hikari looked at the pendulum wall clocks. She observed that each clock showed a different time, and that only the middle clock was correct.

She was looking at it just at the moment it turned five p.m. and it gonged five times.

'I'll wait,' Hikari said, and she picked up the newly poured cup of coffee. For Hikari, who usually drank either instant coffee or her own brew of drip coffee, its taste was difficult to accept as the same drink she knew as coffee. She was pretty sure it must have been the same coffee as the kind she drank when she came to this cafe with Yoji, but she no longer remembered its taste.

My mind was on other things.

Hikari looked up to see the woman in the white dress straight ahead of her, quietly reading a book. The idea of a ghost who went to the toilet was rather odd. But the fact that she was reading a book was no less strange. Hikari wondered what kind of book the woman was reading.

She was turning pages at a timing that suggested she was reading it. Did that, then, mean she was also understanding the content? Were there books that ghosts found interesting and others they didn't? Hikari was growing increasingly curious about the woman in the white dress sitting there before her.

'What is the book you are reading?' Hikari asked the woman in the white dress casually. She wasn't really expecting a reply, and none was forthcoming.

'Kaname likes novels,' replied Nagare in her stead. Hikari thought it odd that he had referred to the ghost by name, but what caught her interest more was what the ghost liked to read.

'How do you know that?'

'When she was alive . . . Oh . . . er.'

'What?'

Nagare had cut himself short with a swallowing gulp followed by regretful mumbling. Judging his reaction when he saw Kazu, it must have been an uncomfortable topic to discuss with her standing there. But Hikari had clearly heard, *When she was alive*.

She also noted that Nagare referred to the woman as Kaname. This Kaname must have had some connection with the cafe. Based on Nagare's reaction, it must have been a delicate topic. But the more secret something is, the more people want to know about it.

Just when Hikari was about to ask, *Who is Kaname?*—

Flap.

It was the sound of a book closing. The woman in the white dress stood up slowly and silently. Hikari's reflex was to stiffen her shoulders and brace herself.

She stood up! The ghost has legs!

Without audible footsteps, the woman in the white dress passed close by petrified Hikari, walked out of the entrance and turned right towards the toilet.

'The seat is vacant.'

'Eh?'

Having been distracted while watching the woman in the dress, Hikari only just noticed Kazu standing before her.

'Will you be sitting there?'

'Yes, of course!' Hikari replied loudly.

'All right. But before you do so, there is one more important rule that I need to explain.'

'There is another important rule?'

'Yes.'

Hikari was curious as to who the woman in the white dress was. But more important now was going back to meet Yoji. After a little pause, she asked, 'What rule are you talking about?'

'After you sit down in the chair, I will pour you a cup of coffee.'

'Coffee again? But you just gave me some.'

Hikari pointed to the cup of coffee placed in front of her.

'It will be a different coffee from that one.'

'. . . Oh, OK.'

Since entering the cafe, Hikari had already drunk one cup of coffee. She had just taken her first sip of her second cup, and only planned to finish it because it would be wasteful not to.

A third cup . . .

She didn't hate coffee. Nevertheless, the idea of having to drink a third cup was unappealing.

Sapped of expression, Hikari gave a little sigh.

'OK. Go on,' she prompted Kazu, so that she would explain the rule.

'The time you spend back in the past will be limited, from when I pour you a coffee until that coffee goes cold. Most importantly, you must drink the entire cup of coffee before it goes cold.'

'Before it goes cold?'

Hikari placed her hand on the cup in front of her. Maybe five or six minutes had passed since it had been refilled, but it was still warm. Maybe several minutes remained before it went cold. Which probably meant her time back in the past would be about fifteen to twenty minutes. She thought that would be sufficient time to accept Yoji's proposal and return. 'OK, I understand,' she replied. It didn't seem such an important rule. The fact that you could not change the present stood out as the bigger issue.

'So, I just have to drink all the coffee before it goes cold, right?'

Hikari had no problem accepting this rule. Drinking all of it before it went cold was a surprisingly simple ask. Hikari picked up her second cup of coffee and took two sips to check. It still wasn't lukewarm, but it was not too hot to gulp down in one go. She was told to drink it all before it went cold, but she wondered, how could someone not finish it?

'By the way, what happens if I don't drink it all?' She was curious, so she asked.

Kazu did not provide an immediate reply. 'If you don't finish it . . .' She paused awkwardly.

'If I don't finish it?'

Then what?

Hikari raised her eyebrows despairingly as she waited for the reply.

'Then it is your turn to become a ghost and constantly occupy the chair.'

'What?'

Hikari looked over to the entrance where the woman in the white dress had left for the toilet and then slowly returned her gaze to Kazu, who was staring expressionlessly at the seat where the woman in the white dress – or rather the ghost – had been sitting.

Wait a minute, I'll be risking my life?

She hadn't realized how big a risk was attached to these rules for going back in time. Suddenly, she was mindful of a serious question.

Until the coffee is cold? Isn't that too vague?

Hikari put her hand against the cup in front of her one more time to check how cold the coffee was.

Hey, what?

No more than a few minutes ago she had been feeling its warmth, but now it was definitely cold.

Unbelievable! When did that happen?

How cold was cold? Suddenly, Hikari had no idea. If the cup felt cold, was that the end of it? In the summer, a coffee gone cold would still be lukewarm.

Just as Hikari was getting increasingly confused, Kazu asked, 'What would you like to do?'

The meaning of her simple, casually delivered question was clear: now that you understand there is a risk that you will turn into a ghost, do you still wish to return to the past?

She was also offering her one last chance to bail out. *If I want to quit, now's the time.*

On hearing this, Hikari reassessed her feelings one more time. She had decided to go back in time for two reasons.

First, she wanted to find out if Yoji's *I've met someone else* was true.

But then again, even if it was true that he had met another woman, it would not have happened for Yoji at the time he proposed to her that day, so it was irrelevant.

Which was why she was planning to accept his proposal. She wanted to do so for Yoji's benefit.

I want to tell him properly how I feel.

It was also for her own benefit. But to do so at the risk of becoming a ghost was too much. She just needed to drink the whole cup of coffee before it went cold. But the vagueness of the *before getting cold* rule was frightening to her. She could get so caught up in the conversation that she would miss that moment of change from *cooling* to *cold*. That temperature boundary might be just one degree, or one-tenth of a degree. The more she thought about it, the more difficult it was to answer.

But if I don't go to see him now, I might regret it more.

Hikari gulped down the second cup of coffee in front of

her. It had gone cold. She stared into the empty cup. She had assumed it was still warm. But when she went to gulp it down, it was thoroughly cold. She hadn't known its temperature.

But now, with this stark realization that the coffee was cold, the time that coffee took to cool seemed vaguer and shorter than she had imagined. She realized then and there that she couldn't rely on her own sense of time. Perhaps time itself was not even absolute, but relative.

So, she reached a conclusion. *I just need to keep holding the cup in my hand and gulp it down as soon as it feels lukewarm.*

Hikari placed the cup on the saucer. 'I think,' she said as she slowly got up, 'I want to see him one more time and properly tell him how I feel, face to face.'

Saying these words made her feel more resolved.

I don't want to regret it again.

She had thought she needed to tell herself a list of reasons to justify going back, when in fact she didn't need one.

I want to see Yoji whatever the risk.

That was all that was needed.

'Very well,' Kazu said as she swung round and headed off to the kitchen.

'I can sit down, right?' Hikari asked Nagare, who had been silently watching her from the counter.

'Yes, of course,' he replied with a courteous hand gesture. Hikari bit her lip and stood in front of the chair that would take her back in time. She felt her heart beat faster. Just sitting down surely wouldn't sweep her off to the past, but still, she didn't know what would happen. She carefully slid between the table and the chair and slowly sat down.

'. . .'

Nothing happened. It felt like sitting in any regular chair. One difference that she did notice was that the whole chair felt a little cold. In fact, it wasn't just the chair. As her initial apprehension dissolved, she began to sense a chilly air engulfing her immediate vicinity.

This is where the ghost was sitting.

No sooner had the thought occurred than a chill ran down her spine.

Who knows, maybe I will end up having to sit here for ever.

As that image entered Hikari's mind, she closed her eyes and shook her head to dispel it. Kazu returned from the kitchen.

In her hands was a tray bearing a pure white cup and a silver kettle. Standing beside Hikari in the time-travelling chair, Kazu cleared away the cup that the woman in the dress had used and placed the pure white cup in front of Hikari.

'If you're ready, I will now pour your coffee.'

'Yes, I'm ready.'

'The time available to you while back in the past will be from when I pour the coffee into this cup until the moment it goes cold.'

'OK.'

When she heard this just earlier, Hikari assumed she would have maybe fifteen to twenty minutes before the coffee cooled. But after knowing the risk of not drinking it all in time, she was seeing things quite differently. She was feeling pressure to gulp it down before ten minutes at maximum, no, she should do it as soon as possible. With that on her mind, she observed Kazu holding out something to her. It looked like a stirrer. Ten centimetres in length.

What is that? Hikari asked Kazu with her eyes.

'If you put this in the cup, like that, it will sound a warning before the coffee gets cold,' Kazu replied as she put the stirrer-like object into the cup.

'This will tell me when the coffee is about to go cold?'

'Yes.'

Well, you could have told me that such a convenient thing existed a little earlier. Give me back the time I spent worrying just now! Hikari swallowed her urge to say these words.

'I see,' she replied simply.

But Hikari knew that even if she had blurted out her frustrations, this waitress would not have changed her expression; there was no ill intent. If she was honest, Hikari was now feeling a lot better.

Worrying about how long it would take for the coffee to cool down was her greatest problem, and now she realized that all she needed to do was to drink it when the alarm sounded.

'Are you ready?'

In response, Hikari took a deep breath. 'All right, I'm ready. Please proceed,' she replied.

As soon as she heard Hikari's reply, Kazu nodded, and took hold of the silver kettle. Instantly, there was tension in the air.

Hikari realized suddenly that her clenched fists were trembling.

I'm scared.

She should have been fully prepared. But it was not a fear of becoming a ghost. She was afraid of meeting a dead person. It was difficult to imagine how it would feel to cast her eyes upon someone who was deceased. She squeezed her eyes shut and bit her lip. Observing her like that, Kazu slowly lifted the kettle and said, 'Before the coffee gets cold.'

The coffee poured slowly from the kettle into the cup. Hikari's eyes opened slightly as she watched it do so. As the cup gradually filled with coffee, a single plume of steam unexpectedly began rising from it.

The steam kept rising towards the ceiling, never disappearing. Hikari thought she was just watching the steam as it rose. But something didn't seem right.

What?

She suddenly noticed her surroundings were beginning to shimmer and warp. Overcome with the feeling that her own body was not her own, she gasped. The ceiling was strangely close. It was only then that Hikari realized that she was not just watching the steam rise but floating as one with it.

This can't be happening!

It wasn't just the looming ceiling, either. Her surroundings had started streaming down around her. In a kaleidoscopic spectacle, many past happenings at the cafe appeared from above and disappeared below.

I'm really going back in time!

Hikari closed her eyes again. If she was honest, she felt confused by the situation, afraid as well.

But it was her chance to see Yoji once more. Just thinking about it shallowed her breathing and made her fidgety and restless.

I'm nervous.

She remembered this nervousness. This was the nervousness she had before she started dating Yoji.

Back in elementary school, I was teased by the boys in my class when I cut my hair short.

Because of that bitter memory, for a long time, I never again cut it short. I wouldn't go as far as to say I was traumatized by the experience, but it was still enough to make me averse to getting such haircuts.

But one day, that changed.

I really cut it!

I was poking my tongue out at myself in the mirror. It was all due to a fortune-telling bit on morning TV. The lucky word in love was 'haircut'. This commentary on how a makeover can improve your love life had spurred me into action.

The thing was, I had my eye on one of the guys who my girl friends and I were hanging out with at the clue-solving gatherings. His name was Ryo Ninomiya. He was a tall and slender sporty type. I heard he played volleyball in junior high and high school. Wanting to attract Ninomiya's attention some-how, I took the plunge and cut my hair short.

But when the six of us got together for the first time after a while, his only comment was, 'Oh, you cut your hair short?'

Oh . . .

I was reliving my original haircut trauma. This time, I wasn't teased. Maybe he didn't mean his comment to sound negative. I know, I know.

It's just that because I was hoping for *it's cute*, or *it suits you*, hearing what he said was enough to make me regret cutting it.

Why did I have to cut it?

I tried my best to smile and not show my feelings. But I was unable to enjoy the rest of the day. The more I laughed, the less and less fun it got. I found myself fiddling with my now-much-shorter hair.

I wasn't sure why. It wasn't as if my hair was going to grow any time soon. I felt ashamed of my ulterior motives inspired by silly fortune-telling. All I could do was feel sad, my only response was to laugh.

'You look good with short hair too.'

The speaker was Yoji. I'll never forget it. It was on the way home that day. His words were like a gentle caress to my fragile heart, so full of kindness and concern for me. By laughing so hard, I had actually been sending out an SOS. And by the end of the day, when it seemed no one had come to my rescue, I even thought, *This is no fun, I don't want to hang out with these people any more.*

Come to think of it, losing my sense of belonging in groups

had been a recurrent theme for me in my life until then. That's why Yoji's words saved me that day.

A year passed, and my hair returned to its original length. I'm not sure exactly when, but at some point, the others in our group had become couples. One day, after the clue-solving game was over, the other two couples went their separate ways and Yoji and I found ourselves alone together.

Normally at this point in the day, Yoji would first disappear into one station, and then I would walk alone to another station, a short distance away. But that day, Yoji said, 'I don't have anything to do right now,' and walked with me towards my station. It was Christmas and one of those rare years that it snowed. The snow was crunching with each of Yoji's steps. I stepped in the snow next to him. I tried not to walk too far apart from him. I made sure not to get too close. The ground was snowy enough that I might lean on him if I wasn't careful, and I was thinking I would like that. All I was seeing was my own feet trudging through the snow.

'Long suits you too,' said Yoji suddenly without warning.

'What?'

I turned to see Yoji shrug his shoulders while exhaling white breath, looking only ahead.

'Your hair.'

'Oh . . . Oh right.'

I clenched a strand of my grown hair.

'Doesn't that mean you don't care, whichever?' I said in a way that was deliberately provoking. When I say provoking, I mean, I was kind of fishing for a reply.

'Sure. Either one looks good.'

'Either one?'

'I like both.'

'I see.'

'Yeah.'

'Thank you.'

It was exactly the answer I was fishing for. We laughed quietly as we stamped through the snow. I was happy. He had remembered that day, a year ago. The day I was hurt, and then saved.

Yoji must have been waiting – for my hair to grow. He likes to pay that kind of attention to detail.

Later, I heard he was planning to ask me out, but I knew that already.

That's why I regret it.

He even proposed to me in this cafe. He actually put it out there for me to accept. But I was taking it for granted that we would be together, which was so spoilt of me. I never thought the relationship would end. But it did. If this is a second chance, I want to take it to tell Yoji just how much he meant to me. Even if nothing can change the present.

Hikari was no longer certain how long she had been watching time stream down around her. She felt it had both been a long time and just a brief moment. Hikari thought that if it were true that people saw their life flash before their eyes when they were dying, it would probably look something like the kaleidoscopic show she witnessed.

Oh . . .

She was suddenly aware of Yoji.

He was sitting in front of her, but at the adjacent table. It put an unnatural distance between them. For her to be sitting at the place where the woman in the white dress, who had been sitting behind Hikari a year ago, seemed a very strange situation indeed. But stranger yet was Yoji, who was supposed to be dead, being there right in front of her.

'Yoji!'

Forgetting the rules, Hikari automatically went to stand up. If she were to stand up, then the very moment she did, she would be brought back to the present. But her reunion with Yoji had left her mind blank.

In the nick of time, Yoji held up his palm and shouted, 'Wait! You can't stand up!'

'What?'

For a moment, Hikari couldn't understand why Yoji had shouted so loudly, and with such panic. But then she remembered the rules.

'Oh!' she cried and immediately returned her weight to her bottom. If Yoji hadn't warned her she would have come this far only to be forcefully returned to the future having accomplished nothing.

'That was close.'

Yoji wiped his forehead melodramatically.

'What?'

Once again, Hikari was thrown for a loop by what had just happened.

Yoji warned me not to stand up. He must know I'm from the future.

Hikari went into a panic. Even if Yoji knew everything there was to know about the rules of this cafe, there would be no way for him to know that Hikari, sitting in this seat, was from the future.

How could he?

Yet just now, Yoji had definitely stopped her from standing up. Why, if not because he knew she was from the future? And he had done it without hesitation.

'Um, perhaps . . .'

Hikari looked askingly at Kazu behind the counter: *You told him?*

Kazu, however, was unresponsive to Hikari's gaze. Acting as if she had not even noticed, she walked into the kitchen.

'Hey – hey . . .'

Hikari's voice trailed off. She had somehow expected Kazu to behave that way. Even if she had properly asked Kazu at that time, she no doubt would have bluntly replied, 'That's not possible.' After all, someone would need to see into the future to know Hikari's arrival. So it was something not even Kazu could have predicted. That was just simple reasoning.

How did Yoji know I was from the future?

When she looked back at Yoji, he had got up from his seat and was coming to her table. With her mind stuck trying to explain what was happening, she forgot entirely what she had planned to say to him. As soon as he came over, Yoji sat opposite her without hesitation. Their eyes met.

Hikari was looking up at him nervously, but for some reason, he was smiling broadly.

What? Is he going to propose to me now?

No sooner than she thought it, she knew that couldn't be it.

No, it can't be. If I remember correctly, Yoji didn't have the composure to smile like this just before he proposed.

Hikari could not work out why Yoji would be smiling as he sat in front of her.

'So, um . . .'

Still confused, Hikari started talking. First she needed to know if *now* was before or after the proposal. If it was before, she could just accept the ring he presented to her. But if it was after, that wouldn't be so easy.

She would have to explain why she turned down the proposal the first time – and do so convincingly, at that. Even if the present wasn't going to change, she didn't want to have come this far only to make things weird between her and Yoji.

There's no time to waste.

'How did you know I was from the future?'

The coffee gets cold fast. I can't beat around the bush.

She gulped. Her heartbeat was quickening under her shallow breaths.

There is nothing I might say that would change the present. I have no influence.

Knowing that had not stopped her growing anxiety. She

was operating to her own agenda, and the conversation would perhaps be troublesome for Yoji. But he seemed fine with her abrupt question. More than fine, in fact.

'I've been waiting for you,' he replied happily.

'What?'

'I've been waiting for you to come from the future.'

Hikari was struggling to come to terms with what Yoji was saying.

'Waiting? . . . For me?'

'Yeah.'

'I don't understand. Why would you do that?'

'I told you that I'll be waiting – if you remember.'

Hikari tilted her head, unsure of when Yoji was talking about.

'Look, it's just a short time ago for me.'

A short time ago?

'In response to my proposal, you said you wanted to concentrate on your work for a bit. Don't you remember?'

My work?

Hikari gazed into space. The wooden ceiling fan was rotating, and the three large pendulum clocks were ticking away the hours distinctly.

'Oh.'

On that day, indeed, Yoji said he would wait.

But that . . .

'What? . . . Wait! . . . Is that what you meant when you said you'd be waiting?'

I thought he meant he'd wait until I was content at work!

'Did you mean that you would wait here, in this cafe, for me to come from the future?'

'I sure did.'

Yoji's immediate response left Hikari lost for words. She could only open and close her mouth.

'You may think I'm lying, but I'm not. It's the reason why I brought you to this cafe in the first place. I thought that if my proposal didn't go well, I could wait here for you to come from the future.'

'That's so crazy.'

'All right then, let me ask you this: in your future, I'm already dead . . . am I right?'

Yoji said the unspeakable without changing his expression. He sounded like he was asking if she had a good time at a party he couldn't attend.

'What? . . . What are you saying? . . .' Her voice wavered.

Her eyes began simmering as her anger seethed. She didn't have the strength of heart to answer yes to that question. How dare he ask her such a question, to which he knew she could not reply. She was trembling, and her teeth started chattering.

'I'm sorry, I'm sorry.'

Yoji smiled apologetically. Hikari couldn't understand how he could be so jovial.

Yoji brought me here because he knew he was going to die.

'And? What did I say at that time?'

'What time are you talking about?'

'When I leave you.'

'Your plans have extended that far?'

'Yeah, I will leave you if I know for sure my condition is worsening.'

For Hikari it was the past, but for Yoji it was what would become. It saddened Hikari to hear the future tense. It was difficult to believe, but if what he said was true . . .

I was only ever thinking about myself.

Hikari closed her eyes in regret of past things she wasn't proud of.

'So, what did I say?'

Yoji looked into Hikari's face with great interest.

'You said you had met someone else.'

'So, I went with that one!' he shouted, loudly enough to echo, as he swung back in his chair.

Hikari observed Yoji's reaction with a frosty expression.

'I've thought about it a lot.'

'About what?'

'What reason to give to break up. One idea was to tell you I lost this, and then have a big fight over it.'

Yoji pulled up his left sleeve to reveal a watch with a leather strap. A birthday present from her. She remembered spending a week looking in different shops after work, not knowing which watch would best suit him. If he had told her he'd lost it, Hikari thought she might ask where he lost it, but she probably wouldn't have got into a fight over it.

'Can you believe I was even considering announcing I was deep in debt, or asking you to buy into my new network business?'

Yoji was laughing to himself, as if he thought he must have been crazy to come up with such things.

'I also thought of just suddenly disappearing without even contacting you.'

After saying that, he looked at Hikari with a sad smile. She thought he was most likely leaning towards that break-up strategy at this moment.

'But I chose that excuse. I told you I met someone else. Hmm. I see.'

Yoji nodded his head in agreement. He seemed to be convincing himself of its merits. Perhaps he was relieved that he wouldn't be choosing to ghost Hikari.

He continued, 'So, how did you take it when I told you I had met someone else, even though I told you earlier that I would wait?'

'I was too stunned to respond, actually,' Hikari replied honestly.

'Yeah, I suppose so.'

Yoji gave another breathy laugh. It was now quite clear that he must have given much thought to getting Hikari to come here after learning of his death.

Hikari's frown was signalling frustration.

'Why didn't you tell me?'

'About my illness?'

'You should have told me.'

'If I had told you, how could you not say yes?'

I can't breathe. He's right. If he had told me about his illness when he proposed, how could I have refused? . . . I wasn't ready to get married, and I didn't feel confident I could live with Yoji for the rest of my life. I just used my work as an excuse . . . But if he had told me about his illness, I probably would have said yes . . . perhaps out of sympathy. It would have stopped me making my own choice. How could I have said no . . . If I had, I would have been left with the burden of heavy regret long after Yoji's death, forever wondering why I didn't just marry him back then.

The decision would have cursed her.

That was precisely what Yoji had foreseen. He knew Hikari well enough to know that she would have been stuck in that curse.

'That's why I thought I would wait.'

Yoji was waiting for me to come to see him on my own accord . . . I wouldn't have come here if he was just that guy who broke up by saying he'd met someone else. Something inside me . . . that I can't put my finger on . . . has brought me here. Part of that might be my regret that I didn't tell him how I feel, and part also might be my wish to hear the truth.

'Wasn't there any other way?'

'I don't know, maybe. If I hadn't known about this cafe, maybe I wouldn't have been able to keep my illness a secret. I might have asked you to marry me . . . even if it meant ignoring your feelings. But if I did, I'm sure I would come to regret it before I die.

'The closer I came to death, the less I would trust your feelings. Every time I would see you looking glum, I would imagine all kinds of things. I might even accuse you of marrying me out of pity because I'm dying.

'I'd hate that. I didn't want that to happen. I just want to make you happy . . . I would have just wanted you to be happy.'

'But if I doubted you, I think my heart would be muddied, and I was afraid it would make it harder to be at peace with dying. So instead, I put my hope in you deciding to come here to meet me.'

'Oh . . .'

'Look, I'm sorry,' Yoji said, concealing his eyes with his hands. The table top was slightly wet.

'I didn't mean to say this. I kind of blew it.'

Watching Yoji look up and sniff heavily, Hikari thought, *The rules of this cafe are so cruel.*

No matter how you try, you cannot change the present. Yoji knew that rule – that's why he was crying. Her being here could only mean he would not escape death.

But still, part of me is glad that I came back to the past. If I hadn't, I would have lived my whole life not knowing Yoji's real thoughts, or rather, his suffering . . . He had told me he would wait, but then dumped me, saying there was another woman . . . I had even started telling myself that, to try to forget him.

'What were you going to do if I found someone else after we broke up?'

In truth, this wasn't even what Hikari wanted to communicate. There were much more important things. She even knew exactly what Yoji would say. But she asked anyway.

'In that case, of course, you should be happy together with that person. Why should you care about a man who met another woman even though he said he would wait?'

Ah, yes. His answer was just as I expected.

At this point it was difficult to tell if Yoji was laughing while crying or crying while laughing.

'You are really selfish; do you know that?'

I don't mean it. Why am I still saying spiteful things to him, even now that I know how much he had thought about me.

'I'm sorry.'

You shouldn't be apologizing. I should be doing that.

But.

'I still wish you had told me. Yes, I might have married you out of pity. Even so, I wanted to suffer together with you. I may have had many sleepless nights thinking that you might die, and I might have discovered many things I don't like about you. But even so, I still wish I had been with you. I wanted to share your feelings – your real feelings.'

'I'm sorry.'

'What am I meant to do now? What am I going to do?'

Hikari covered her face with her hands and started to wail. Yoji kept his eyes on her as he gently reached forward and placed his hand on the side of the coffee cup. Momentary seriousness spread over his face, and he bit his lip tightly.

Then he pulled a small ring box out of his jacket pocket and said, 'Here,' as he placed it beside the cup.

The ring box came into view through the gaps between her fingers, causing even more tears to gush from Hikari's eyes.

'I want you to take it.'

'But you know the present won't change?'

'I know.'

'Even if I say, "Yes," you know there can never be a wedding?'

'Yes. That's OK.'

'You're so sneaky. How could I say no to this?'

'Yes. I'm sorry. It seems you had to suffer whichever I chose. I'm really sorry. I'm sure this is just me being selfish. I know that . . . But still.'

'You're so selfish.'

'Hikari, will you . . .'

'Just too selfish!'

'. . . marry me.'

Yoji's eyes were the most beautiful she had ever seen. She wanted to say yes, but she couldn't. Because even if she did, she had to return to the present. Then Yoji would live with past-Hikari, who knew nothing.

That's too cruel.

'I hate all this,' Hikari said, looking up at the ceiling. She put her hands on her eyelids in a futile attempt to stem her flowing tears.

'Most of all, I hate that you're going to die.'

When she heard the news of Yoji's death, it caused mind fog. While everyone else was crying at the funeral, only she couldn't.

She was still in shock from him telling her he had met someone else – even though he said he would wait. She had believed those words, so she was determined not to cry for that guy who had selfishly broke up with her, and then selfishly died.

But Hikari had realized her true feelings.

I don't want you to die.

'I wanted to marry properly . . .'

Hikari wailed like a child.

'That's your answer? That's very you.'

Yoji's reaction was still to laugh.

I'm being stubborn. I'm not being honest. I know.

Yoji took the ring from its case and grasped Hikari's left hand.

'For the next six months, I can't tell you what happened today. Because of this cafe's rule, even if I try to tell you, you won't listen, or even if you do, you won't believe me. Still, I'm glad I got to know how you felt. It made me happy. I don't regret meeting you; I don't regret wanting to marry you; and I don't regret proposing to you. So, I'm going to live with a smile.'

Yoji then slowly placed the ring on Hikari's left ring finger.

Beep, beep, beep, beep, beep . . .

'Oh.'

The stirrer in the cup was beeping. It was doing its job, sounding an alarm before the coffee got cold.

'I guess that's your time.'

'Yoji.'

'You'd better drink up.'

Hikari held the ring on her ring finger to her chest as if hugging it. She was reluctant to reach for the cup.

'Quickly.'

'No.'

Why am I so stubborn? How annoying I must seem! Even now, I'm still causing him trouble. I don't want to drink, even though I know he will suffer if I don't.

'Oh boy,' Yoji sighed loudly.

But even now, he smiled. Maybe he had even envisaged that this might happen.

'You know if you don't go back to the future, I'll have to deal with two Hikaris in this world, right? . . . If that happened, the Hikari already here will be jealous of you having the ring, and you'd boast about it to her, wouldn't you? . . . Please don't do this, I can't afford to buy another ring this expensive. I'll keep it a secret that I gave you the ring, so please, go back to the future. Like this.'

Yoji made a praying-hands gesture. He must have been well aware what would happen once the coffee was cold. How could he not know when he had even predicted Hikari's arrival from the future?

If he told her to leave firmly, she would probably stubbornly stay.

But how could she not leave when Yoji was making jokes for her, even though he knew he was going to die.

This thought made it plain to see, she would regret it if she didn't return.

Beep, beep, beep, beep, beep . . .

Beep, beep, beep, beep, beep . . .

A second warning. This time, it sounded more insistent. Time was about to run out.

'Ahhh . . . Ah!'

She yelled, trying to break out of this emotional pull. But still she couldn't make up her mind.

'Ahhh . . . Ah!'

While looking up at the ceiling, she shouted one more time, even louder.

'If you insist, I have no choice,' she screamed.

Wiping her tears with the back of her hand, she picked up the cup. The coffee seemed noticeably colder than the one she was served before returning to the past. This one could very well be on the verge of going cold.

There was no more time.

'Be nice to me back here until the very last minute we part.'

'Of course.'

Oh.

Something about what she had said just then struck her.

My parting from Yoji was sudden. The reason for that may have been my request right now. I see. There was a good reason for Yoji's unreasonable betrayal. I may have been the one who caused it. At that time, I just imagined what Yoji's actions meant and got annoyed over that.

Hikari giggled.

'So long,' she said, and drank her coffee in one gulp.

A strong sour taste lingered in the back of her throat. As soon as she returned the cup to the saucer, she began to go all billowy from head to toe.

In the next instant, she found herself beginning to float up while the scenery around her began to flow down.

'Oh.'

She found herself floating about two metres in the air, looking down at Yoji almost from the ceiling. She still felt her body, but when she tried to move what she thought was her hand, nothing was there but vapour.

'Yoji!'

'Hikari.'

Yoji's voice sounded so kind, even at this moment.

'Thank you, Yoji!

'Thank you for meeting me!

'Thank you for liking me!

'Thank you for waiting for me!

'In the end, I couldn't do anything for you, but I'm still glad I came!'

'Yeah.'

'Thank you for proposing to me! Thank you, heaps and heaps!'

'No, thank you! It was only for that short time until the coffee got cold . . .'

'What?'

Yoji's voice sounded choppy, like a radio with a bad signal.

'. . . but I was happy to be married to you.'

With those words, Yoji's voice and all sign of him vanished in the flow of time.

'Yoji!'

Hikari's voice could no longer reach him.

But still, she continued to call his name.

The next thing she knew, the woman in the white dress was standing in front of her. Her hands that were steamy vapour had now returned to normal.

'That is my seat,' said the woman in an oddly low voice.

'Oh, sorry.'

Hikari hurriedly relinquished the seat.

When she placed her hand on the table to stand up, she heard a hard click. On the third finger of her left hand, she still had the ring that Yoji gave her.

'Oh!'

It hadn't been a dream. Not that she had any doubt. Still, if it wasn't for the ring on her ring finger, who was to say it wasn't. She had to admit it felt unbelievable, even now.

But the ring is real.

It was her proof that she had accepted Yoji's proposal. The lie he had told about meeting another woman, and the steps he had taken to be kind to her until they parted, they had all been the fulfilment of his promise to her. The ring on her ring finger created an invisible thread that linked Yoji and Hikari through time.

'How was it?' Kazu asked Hikari as she was clearing the empty cup.

Moments after asking, she had already disappeared into the kitchen. All that could be heard was the tick-tock tock-tick of the three pendulum clocks. The woman in the dress had once again commenced reading in the seat that takes you through time.

135

Nagare was standing behind the counter with his arms folded.

I'm back.

Hikari closed her eyes and could still see images of Yoji, who she had been with just earlier.

Yoji had stayed laughing till the end.

Hikari felt she was about to cry again, but she bit her lip and held it in.

I'm going to live with a smile too.

Hikari picked up her coat hanging on the back of the chair and walked to the cash register.

'Thank you,' said Kazu as a farewell.

'On the contrary, thank you,' replied Hikari in return.

I'm glad I came.

Hikari looked around the cafe again.

When she first came here, she thought she would never return to what she had considered a dingy, slightly creepy cafe. But now, it kind of glowed.

'Oh, I almost forgot,' she said suddenly. 'Can you guess what Yoji said to bring me here that day?' she asked Nagare and Kazu.

Just one of Nagare's thread-thin eyes widened, and he uttered his usual 'Umm.'

Kazu stayed silent, tilting her head slightly.

Hikari giggled. She knew it was a funny question to ask. It must have sounded like it came out of the blue, and she was sure it didn't matter to either of them.

Nevertheless, she wanted to tell them.

'Yoji said . . . "I know a cafe that will make you happy, would you like to go?"'

On that day, those words just gave me a bad feeling. But now, I feel differently. Yoji must have already imagined how I would be feeling now. And it turned out exactly how he said it would.

'Oh, really?' replied Kazu with a faint smile as she retreated to the kitchen.

'He sounded like a wonderful boyfriend.'

'Oh, he's not.'

Hikari crisply refuted Nagare's response.

She presented her left hand to Nagare, making him blink repetitively.

A silver ring was gleaming on her ring finger.

'He's my husband.'

'Oh, I stand corrected,' said Nagare as his thread-thin eyes arched beamingly and he nodded his head courteously to Hikari's highly spirited declaration.

CLANG-DONG

Hikari left the cafe, and stamping through the crunchy snow, she walked towards the station.

It was Christmas again.

She remembered when she and Yoji had walked together that night.

CRUNCH . . . CRUNCH . . . CRUNCH . . .

IV

The Daughter

Michiko Kijimoto was entirely fed up.

Hadn't she purposely chosen to go to university in Tokyo – far away from the little port town of Yuriage in the city of Natori, in Miyagi Prefecture – to escape her father's annoying interference? Yet there he was, looking back at her disapprovingly.

His name was Kengo Kijimoto.

They were in a cafe called Funiculi Funicula, two stations from the university. Michiko had been to this second-basement cafe once before. On that occasion, she had found its dim lighting and absence of windows depressing.

I never imagined I'd come back here.

But that actually was the reason she chose it to meet up with Kengo. If she had chosen a cafe she frequented, she might have bumped into a friend. She didn't want her friends to see her country bumpkin father.

'Are you eating properly?' His voice was hoarse and intimidating.

She had got a similar ear-bashing from that voice many times before. Not that it had bothered her so much while her mother was alive.

Michiko's mother was a round-faced woman who laughed often and praised well. She had baked cakes for birthdays, had taken countless photos of Michiko dressed up in a kimono during the Shichi-Go-San festival and displayed them all over the room.

If Michiko scored one hundred per cent on a test, her mother would come home with a huge uneatable amount of *takoyaki* (octopus balls), which Michiko so loved. Even when Michiko protested that she couldn't eat any more, her mother just laughed and said, 'Just one more, one more!'

Michiko loved her mother.

But Mum has gone now.

When life with just Kengo began, there were no more cakes on birthdays, no more commemorative photos, and no more treats of takoyaki to celebrate a good test score.

The only thing that increased was the nagging.

'Do your homework.'

'Hurry up and go to bed.'

'Don't stay up late messing around.'

'Choose your friends wisely.'

'Don't wear that.'

'No, that's no good.'

'I can't allow that.'

Even though she had left her hometown of Yuriage to go to university in Tokyo to escape from that spell . . . The father she hated was sitting in front of her.

'Are you going to lectures and studying?'

Michiko sighed loudly and turned her head away.

'Michiko.'

'What are you saying? I should be doing so because you're paying a lot of money for the university fees?'

'Who said anything about that?'

'Well, that's basically what you're saying. All of a sudden, you come to Tokyo and use my university teachers to call me.'

'That's because you . . .'

Michiko glared at him.

That's because I never contacted you once, right?

She knew what he wanted to say.

Kengo mumbled, 'Sorry,' and looked down.

'So, are we done?'

They had been together for just fifteen minutes.

Michiko wanted to leave this irritating space as soon as possible, so she took the souvenir bag Kengo had given her and stood up.

'Michiko.'

Kengo stopped her as she swiftly made her way to the exit.

'What? Was there something else?'

Though I think this back and forth right now is a waste of time.

This time, Michiko bit her tongue, but her emotions were revealed through the lines of her forehead.

Kengo averted his gaze to avoid seeing the look of disgust

on the face looking back at him and said, 'If you have a problem, just tell me, OK? It doesn't matter what it is. Don't keep it to yourself . . .'

BAM!

Suddenly, there was a loud noise in the cafe.

Kengo's eyes widened as he saw the souvenirs meant for Michiko scattered at his feet.

She had thrown the entire bag to the floor.

'That's what I hate! Don't you see? I'm almost twenty, do you understand? I'm not a child! I want you to stop meddling in my life like this! Why do you think I went to university in Tokyo? It's because I don't like you interfering like this.'

As the only customers in the restaurant were Michiko, Kengo and the woman in the white dress at the back of the room, Michiko did not hesitate to raise her voice in anger.

She knew it would hurt him. *I'd actually rather it did hurt him*, she thought.

'Why don't you get it?'

She had no sympathy for her interfering father, who was constantly preaching to her about what he thought she should or shouldn't do.

She just wanted him out of her sight as soon as possible.

'I'm sorry,' Kengo muttered weakly.

'Just go home.' She could only get annoyed when she saw him sulk in dejection. 'Go home!'

Kengo slowly rose from his chair then crouched down to pick up the souvenirs scattered at his feet. He made the point of brushing off dust that wasn't there and put the custard-filled sponge cake, bamboo-leaf moulded fishcake, the mashed juvenile soybean soft chewy rice, and the pack of takoyaki back into the paper bag, one by one.

They were all things that Michiko liked. He presented the bag to her, but she would not take it.

Kengo looked sadly at Michiko, who had turned away not even making eye contact with him, and then walked out of the cafe with his shoulders slumped.

CLANG-DONG

'. . . and that was six years ago,' said Michiko to conclude her tale as she looked up solemnly.

'Six years ago?'

Ruminating on this was Nagare Tokita, the cafe's owner.

'You're one lousy daughter,' remarked Nana Kohtake, sitting at the counter, in no mood to mince words. She was a nurse who worked at a nearby hospital, and one of the cafe's regulars.

'Ms Kohtake, please.'

'What?'

Nagare silently signalled to Kohtake not to be rude, but instead of making a retraction, she just slurped her coffee.

Michiko, perhaps affected by Kohtake's words, looked apologetic.

'I heard that if I came here, I could go back in time?' she enquired. She had got to the point.

'OK, er . . .'

Stuck for words, Nagare exchanged glances with Kohtake. Their reaction made Michiko feel uneasy.

I guess that means it's not true.

Deep down, she had never really believed it.

But if it was possible, if I could go back . . .

That was the thought that led her here.

There was a reason she wanted, no, *had to* go back.

'It *is* possible to go back, right?'

Her voice was louder than she expected. Nagare just scratched his temple in confusion.

'So, can I?'

She was even more agitated. But Nagare was no more forth-coming. She looked at him grimly.

'What would you do if you could go back?' Kohtake asked.

By her tone, she knew already what Michiko would say next.

'I want to save my father.'

'Save?'

'Yes, just three days after that day in the cafe when I drove my father away, six years ago. The earthquake . . .'

She couldn't say any more. Her regret had never gone away, even after six years.

'If only I hadn't turned him away that day . . .'

On 11 March 2011, Japan's largest earthquake in recorded history occurred. The Great East Japan Earthquake.

The devastation of this disaster was still fresh in the minds of everyone here, even six years on. Nagare was at a loss for words and Kohtake averted her gaze and stayed silent.

Kazu Tokita alone looked at Michiko steadfastly. Kazu was the waitress in the cafe. It was her role to pour the coffee for going back in time. She had a fair complexion with thin almond-shaped eyes, but none of her features were particularly striking.

In short, she was difficult to notice. Michiko certainly hadn't noticed her existence until she was looking at her face to face.

'Please! Take me back to that day when I said those horrible things to my father and drove him away!' repeated Michiko to Kazu, bowing her head deeply.

I want to save Dad.

Her sentiment was painfully obvious to Nagare and Kohtake. But they knew something she didn't – something they were finding difficult to tell her.

Michiko was unaware of a crucial rule about returning to the past.

'Look, there is something you need to know,' said Kazu.

'OK.'

'You can go back. You can go back to the past, but . . .'

'But what?'

'No matter how hard you try when you go back in time, you won't be able to save your father.'

'What?'

'Even if you kept him in Tokyo, you can't change the fact your father will die.'

'Why not?'

'I'm sure you want a good reason, but it is simply the rule.'

Kazu's matter-of-fact tone of voice irritated Michiko.

Even if I can't save my father, why do you have to tell me so dispassionately? Can't you even imagine what I'm feeling coming here after learning I could go back in time? The manager and that other woman, they're strangers to me too, but at least they looked sympathetic when they heard of my father's death.

'How can that be?'

Most frustrating of all was to see Kazu's calm eyes, which were impossible to doubt.

'Then wouldn't that mean there is no point going back?'

Saying it out loud was not going to change anything. She had blurted it out in anger, she couldn't stop herself.

'In a sense, yes,' said Kazu simply, looking down sadly for just a moment.

'. . . Unbelievable.'

Kazu watched Michiko collapse into a chair, then turned away and left for the kitchen. Michiko seemed sapped of all life.

'It's tough news to hear.'

'We understand how you feel.'

But she was no longer hearing Nagare's and Kohtake's comments. Her heart was deflating like a punctured balloon.

She felt like she had started running a full marathon feeling completely prepared and ready, only to be told just before the finish line that the race had been cancelled, and in fact, there never even was a finish line. This outcome seemed so mercilessly one-sided against her.

Michiko had a fiancé. His name was Yusuke Mori, and he had joined the company at the same time as her. They had known each other for three years. It was Yusuke who told her that she could go back in time in this cafe.

Michiko hadn't believed him at first. In fact, she was even angry at him for suggesting such a stupid idea as 'you can go back in time'. At first she dismissed it as a joke. But he insisted it was true, claiming he was told the story by a woman called Fumiko Kiyokawa, who had actually visited the past.

Fumiko Kiyokawa was a systems engineer for a client company that Yusuke dealt with directly, and although still in her twenties, her reputation for successfully pulling off major projects had preceded her, reaching even Michiko's ears.

'I don't think Ms Kiyokawa would lie to me. I didn't tell her about your story, of course, and there's no reason for her to make up such a wild tale. She did mention there were some annoying rules. But if you really can go back in time, why not try?'

'But . . .'

'Why don't you just go back in time and fix things? Like, don't turn him away this time. And get him to stay in Tokyo. If you could do that . . .'

Could I really fix things? Could I relive that day?

These words had ignited hope in Michiko's heart.

The regret she suffered from driving her father away was a trauma that gave her heart palpitations whenever she thought of it. It had taken a lot of courage to enter this cafe. But now it seemed pointless.

Kohtake sat down in the seat opposite Michiko and said, 'Don't be so downhearted. There is nothing you can do about it. It's just the rule.'

But Michiko remained slumped on the table, not moving a muscle.

'Oh, this is hopeless.'

Kohtake shrugged her shoulders and shook her head at Nagare.

CLANG-DONG

'Hello. Welcome.'

A young man in a casual suit entered the room.

'Are you by yourself?'

The young man gave a polite acknowledgement to Nagare's question and walked over to Michiko, who was still slumped on the table.

'Michiko.'

Michiko looked up in response.

'Oh! . . . Yusuke.'

The young man was Yusuke Mori, the one who encouraged Michiko to go back in time.

'I waited outside for ages, but you never came . . .'

'Oh, sorry.'

'No problem.'

When Nagare found out that Yusuke was an acquaintance of Michiko's, he turned to Kohtake and patted his chest as if to say, I'm glad someone came to get her.

Kohtake jutted her chin towards their exchange as if to indicate, It's a bit too early to tell yet.

'So, how did it go? Did you get to meet your father?'

Michiko got up suddenly. Nagare, Kohtake and even Yusuke widened their eyes in surprise.

'I'm sorry.'

'Eh?'

'I can't marry you.'

She took her wallet out of her shoulder bag, put a thousand-yen note on the table, and ran out of the cafe.

'Michiko!'

CLANG-DONG

Just as Yusuke was about to chase after Michiko, Kohtake called out, 'Wait there, mister.'

'What?'

Yusuke looked puzzled to have been suddenly accosted by an unknown woman.

'Um, what?'

'Ms Kohtake?'

Yusuke wasn't the only one who was taken aback. Nagare was frowning.

'Sorry about this.'

Nagare cowered his large body and bowed to Yusuke. However, if Yusuke had really wanted to, he could have ignored Kohtake and chased after Michiko. But he hadn't. He couldn't.

'She didn't go back in time.'

'What?'

'Because she wouldn't be able to save her father even if she did.'

When Kohtake explained Michiko's situation to Yusuke, he let out a small sigh and mumbled, 'I see.'

'What does her not being able to save her father have to do with your not being able to marry?' Kohtake asked in a quiet, calm voice.

Yusuke caught sight of Michiko's handkerchief, which she had left behind on the table.

'She said she couldn't bear it that only she could be happy,' he said in a fading voice, now holding the handkerchief.

'What do you mean?'

Yusuke took a deep breath and began talking in hushed tones.

'For the last six years, she has lived with the constant regret of what she did here, driving her father away like that . . . The tsunami did not hit Yuriage until an hour after the initial quake. So her father was evacuated with the town people, but suddenly he said he was going back to get his bankbook . . .'

'Bankbook?'

'Apparently, the people at the port tried to stop him, saying he should wait till later, but he said, "It's my savings for my daughter for when she gets married," and . . .'

There were no words that could follow. Everyone was having flashbacks of the tragic scenes they witnessed that day on live TV. Kohtake and Nagare were both staring at the floor.

'There's nothing that can be done about that, I guess?'

'What's done is done.'

Some problems of the heart can only be solved by the person concerned. The reason Yusuke hadn't been able to run after Michiko was because he knew that there was no room for him in her emotional plight. Yusuke said nothing more. After quietly bowing his head, he left the cafe.

That evening, after closing time, a man was sitting at a table looking at brochures, showing no sign of leaving. If he was left to his own devices, he probably wouldn't leave. Yet Kazu Tokita was quietly tidying the counter.

The only sound was the ticking of the pendulum clocks.

CLANG-DONG

The doorbell rang, but Kazu didn't give her normal greeting, 'Hello. Welcome.' She simply looked towards the entrance, as if she knew who would be coming in.

'Thanks for the call, Kazu.'

At the door was Kohtake. She was dressed in her nurse's uniform and visibly out of breath. Kazu offered her a glass of water.

'Thank you.'

Kohtake drank it in one gulp.

'Oh, that reminds me.'

After returning the glass, Kohtake went back to the entrance of the cafe.

Voices came from the doorway.

'You're not coming in?'

'Yeah, but . . .'

'Come on, it's fine. Come in,' said Kohtake. Then appearing at the entrance, being pushed forward by Kohtake, was Michiko. She was looking down regretfully.

'I found her halfway down the stairs . . .' Kohtake told Kazu with pleading eyes as she ushered Michiko in.

Kazu looked at Michiko. Instead of the usual, 'Hello. Welcome,' she greeted her with, 'Good evening.' Business hours were over.

'Er, good evening,' Michiko replied.

In the meantime, Kohtake slipped past Michiko and stood beside the man looking at the brochure.

'Mr Fusagi,' Kohtake called out to him. The man called Fusagi glanced up at Kohtake for a moment but returned his gaze to his brochure without saying anything.

'Mr Fusagi, did you get to sit in it today?'

Kohtake's question seemed to grab the attention of the

man called Fusagi. He lifted his head for the first time, looked at the woman in the white dress sitting at the far end of the room, and replied, 'No, I couldn't.'

'So, no luck today?'

'No.'

'It looks like it's past closing time here, so why don't you go home?'

'Oh . . .'

Fusagi glanced over to the cafe's middle pendulum clock. The hands were showing eight-thirty p.m.

'Oh, excuse me.'

He hurriedly put away his brochure and headed to the cash register, where Kazu was waiting. Kohtake observed him with loving eyes.

'How much?'

'Three hundred and eighty yen.'

'There you go.'

'Just the right amount, thank you.'

'Thank you.'

Fusagi left in a hurry.

CLANG-DONG

Kohtake nodded courteously to Kazu, smiled, and said, 'Thanks for the call,' before following Fusagi out.

CLANG-DONG

Only Kazu, Michiko and the woman in the white dress remained in the quiet cafe. Michiko was standing there at a loss, not knowing where to start or what to say.

Abruptly, Kazu asked her, 'You wish to do this anyway?' Michiko had not said anything, but Kazu knew why she had come. *Even if you do go back in time, you cannot save your father. Even knowing that, do you still wish to do it?* That was what Kazu was saying.

Michiko gulped. She didn't know why she was here. She knew she couldn't save her father by going back in time. But not completely. Perhaps she still harboured a faint hope that she could save him.

Maybe, just maybe . . .

That was it.

If Kazu had asked, *Why did you think you would go back to the past?* then as she had no reason to give, Michiko might have abandoned the idea. But she was being pressed with, *Do you wish to do this anyway?*

Hanging her head low, she began muttering, 'After my mother died . . .' She was talking as if to herself. '. . . my father brought me up by himself.

'He worked day and night to pay for me to go to university in Tokyo, but oblivious of his sacrifice, I didn't study much at university and just played around . . .

'I just wanted to leave my hometown and be free. I even saw my father as an annoyance. I never went home and kept ignoring his calls until he came to see me that day.'

Without saying anything, not even to throw in the appropriate word, Kazu just listened quietly.

'I said some awful things to him and drove him away, never imagining something like that would happen. At the very least, I want to apologize. I just want to say sorry to my father.'

When she put it into words, Michiko was surprised how clear it actually was to her – the reason she had decided to return to the cafe.

'Please, let me go back. I want to return to that day when I turned my father away.'

Michiko bowed her head deeply to Kazu.

Flap.

The unexpected noise came from the corner of the room. Turning to the sound, Michiko recognized it was made by a book closing – the one the woman in the white dress had been reading.

It was the first time Michiko had seen the woman's face. It was white, with a stare too glazy to tell where she was looking. But her eyes vaguely resembled those of the waitress in front of her. The strangest thing of all was that the woman was wearing short sleeves at this time of the year, when a coat was needed outside, if not inside.

The woman, paying no attention to Michiko's gaze, stood up slowly and walked silently out of the room, heading towards the toilet.

While Michiko was entranced by the sight of the woman heading off to the toilet, she heard a voice behind her say, 'Very well.'

It was Kazu replying to Michiko's request to take her back to that day. Kazu ushered Michiko to the seat where the woman in the white dress had been sitting and began to explain some of the rules for going back in time.

In addition to the rule Michiko learned earlier in the day, that *no matter how you try, you cannot change the present when back in the past*, she also learned the rules that you can only meet people who have visited the cafe; that there is only one chair in which you can return to the past; that you cannot get up from or move from the chair; and that there is a time limit.

Why so many rules?

Indifferent to Michiko's dismay, Kazu returned from the kitchen with a silver kettle and a white cup on a tray and continued her explanation with a detached air.

'Soon I will pour you a cup of coffee,' she explained while placing the cup in front of Michiko.

'Coffee?' Michiko cocked her head inquisitively. She didn't see the connection between going back in time and coffee.

'The time you may spend back in the past is limited, from the time I pour the coffee until the time the coffee gets cold.'

'What? That short? Was that the time limit you mentioned just now?'

'That's right.'

Michiko was very dissatisfied with this rule. It was too vague and too short. But she knew it must be a rule that she could not say or do anything about. She remembered the firmness of Kazu's tone when she told her earlier that she could not save her father.

'All right, then. What else do I need to know?'

Kazu continued.

'When someone goes to see a lost one, it is often too emotional to say goodbye, especially while faced with a time restraint. So, we have this . . .'

Kazu picked up what looked like a stirrer from the tray and held it out in front of Michiko.

'What's that?'

'By putting it in the cup like this, the alarm will sound before the coffee gets cold. You must drink up your coffee as soon as it rings.'

Kazu put the stirrer-like object into the cup and then picked up the silver kettle.

'So, I just need to drink the coffee when it rings?'

'Yes.'

Michiko took a small deep breath.

I'm going to see my dead father.

Just the thought of it made her chest tighten and her breath become irregular. Would she be able to keep her cool?

They had told her that there was nothing she could do that would change the present, but what if she became distraught and said something about the disaster – about her father dying?

Then how would he feel in the days leading up to his death? She was overwhelmed by her racing thoughts.

'Shall I proceed?' asked Kazu, as if to dispel her misgivings.

Well, whatever, I've already made up my mind. I decided to tell my father I was sorry when she asked earlier whether I wished to do this anyway.

Michiko closed her eyes and took a deep breath.

'Please continue,' she replied.

There was no going back now. In contrast to the determined look in Michiko's eyes, Kazu's expression remained calm and collected as she lifted the kettle.

I'm going to the past. I'm really going.

Michiko could feel the tension build in the air.

'Before the coffee gets cold.'

Kazu's voice rang clearly in the silent room as she started to pour the coffee.

A plume of vapour swirled up from the cup as it filled with coffee. The ceiling rippled and warped.

Am I feeling dizzy?

Michiko watched the trajectory that the plume of vapour was following. But in reality, her own body was floating in the air like vapour. Her surroundings began flowing down around her from the ceiling to the floor.

What the . . . what's going on?

With her head spinning, Michiko's consciousness faded.

Dad . . .

At 2.46 p.m. on Friday 11 March 2011, an earthquake struck off northern Honshu's Sanriku Coast. The largest earthquake ever recorded in Japan, its epicentre was 24 kilometres deep

into the Earth's crust, 130 kilometres east-south-east of Oshika Peninsula.

It had a magnitude of 9.0 on the Richter scale, and the disaster caused by the quake became known as the Great East Japan Earthquake.

In the city of Natori, more than 960 people were killed, including related deaths, and around 11,000 people were forced to evacuate.

The damage from the initial shock was relatively small compared to other earthquakes but what made this one so devastating was the enormous destruction brought about by the tsunami.

The tsunami reached the Natori city neighbourhood of Yuriage at 3.52 p.m., about an hour after the earthquake. It was this delay that led to cases like Kengo's, who had briefly evacuated immediately after the earthquake but returned home only to become a victim of the tsunami.

Kengo and Michiko had lived in a residential area near the Natori City Fire Department's Yuriage Fire Station, and also close by was the shop selling Michiko's favourite 'Yuriage takoyaki', located opposite the Minato Shrine.

The takoyaki sold there were different from those sold elsewhere, as they were generously stuffed with octopus meat and served on bamboo skewers with a sweet and spicy sauce.

They looked like a large skewered dumpling and were more chewy than regular takoyaki.

Ever since she was a young child, Michiko had enjoyed

eating these Yuriage takoyaki, so when she moved to Tokyo and a friend recommended the Osaka-style takoyaki as delicious, she could not even accept them as takoyaki.

Yuriage takoyaki.

It was the food that provoked warm memories of her hometown, even though she had abandoned local life because she didn't like her father's interference.

Michiko awoke to the gravelly sound of coffee beans being ground.

The person grinding them was a girl with cool, nonchalant eyes. Was she a high-school student? Perhaps junior high school? Her pale complexion and sombre expression were somewhat familiar.

Was it the woman in the white dress who had left this seat to go to the toilet? . . . No. She resembled the waitress who had just poured her coffee.

It was more than resemblance. She was clearly the same person.

Michiko hadn't recognized her straight away because her long ponytailed hair was now short.

It seems I've actually returned to six years ago.

Her eyes scurried around the cafe, looking for any other evidence that she had returned to the past. But apart from the girl grinding beans at the counter, she couldn't find anything that made a difference. It was as if time had stopped in this cafe . . .

CLANG-DONG

'Hello. Welcome.'

Kazu's calm voice was at odds with the youthfulness of her appearance. Kengo, Michiko's father, entered the cafe with heavy footsteps.

Michiko's heart leaped.

For six years, she had never forgotten the way Kengo looked on that day.

When he spotted Michiko, he walked over to the table, scratching his head. He nodded apologetically.

'I'm sorry.'

'What for?'

'Haven't you been waiting?'

'Oh, no, it's OK.'

'Really?'

'Yeah.'

Michiko's memories came flooding back.

That day, Michiko had said abrasively, 'I can't believe you called me and then turned up late.'

She also clearly remembered the look on Kengo's face at that moment.

How his face had contorted apologetically as he said, 'I'm sorry.'

Why did I have to speak to him so horribly?

'Can I sit here?'

Kengo put his hand on the seat opposite Michiko.

'Of course.'

As he sat down, Kengo's eyes widened as he looked into Michiko's face.

'What?'

'I was just thinking how all grown-up you seem since I saw you last . . .'

Kengo made a grimacing smile in embarrassment. Six years had passed. Kengo was understandably surprised to find himself looking at the twenty-five-year-old Michiko.

'Oh, do you think?'

As she answered, she noticed the deep wrinkles on Kengo's face and the faint grey hairs on his head. When did he get so old?

She was taken aback that she had not even looked properly at her father's face back then. But Kengo had no way of knowing Michiko's confusion.

'Hello, would you like to order?' asked the youthful Kazu as she served a glass of water.

'Coffee, please.'

'Certainly, sir.'

Having taken Kengo's order, Kazu headed off into the kitchen.

Silence.

She couldn't find the words. What could she say? When she looked into Kengo's eyes, she felt the burn of tears coming on.

Despite her intentions, she couldn't help but look away, which served only to make the atmosphere seem more awkward.

She didn't want him to think she was ignoring him.

I'm sorry.

She felt those words that she had swallowed so many times were about to come out of her mouth.

It was in that moment.

'I know I shouldn't have done it, I'm sorry.'

Kengo was the one to speak first.

'Done what?'

Michiko had no idea why he was apologizing.

She was the one who wanted to apologize.

'Calling the university.'

Michiko remembered how furious she'd been. She hadn't thought her father worried about such things.

'Oh. No, it's OK. It was bad of me not to contact you at all.'

Kengo's stiff expression seemed to relax a little. After her mother's death, Michiko would rebel against him about almost anything, which often led to fights. He was probably expecting she would start a fight.

'Oh, here . . .'

As if suddenly remembering them, Kengo put the paper bag he was holding on the table and from it, he took out a small package.

'I bought these because I know they're your favourite . . . they're cold, I'm afraid.'

Michiko knew what was in the package. It was takoyaki, her favourite. Yuriage takoyaki from her hometown, to be exact.

The same that her mother used to buy her when she was a child – chewy and dumpling-like. As long as she had this, she could always smile.

That day when she drove her father away, she had been inexplicably annoyed to find this takoyaki among the souvenirs scattered on the floor. It seemed to her that he was trying to use the memory of her mother, who she loved, to put himself in good stead.

She had thought it was just cowardly manipulation. And she had even felt disgusted.

But no, it wasn't. I can see that now.

Dad had gone to the trouble to buy these takoyaki to make me happy. But despite all that . . .

'Thank you,' she said in a trembling voice. She couldn't look Kengo in the face properly. To bridge the silence, she brought the cup to her mouth.

It's lukewarm.

She could not begin to perceive how much time she had left before the coffee would be cold.

Why on earth did I come here?

She wanted to apologize to her father. That feeling had not changed. But what exactly did she want to apologize for?

I'm sorry I was so selfish about wanting to go to university in Tokyo.

I'm sorry I've only ever complained since Mum died.

I'm sorry I was so cold to you, even when you waited up until I came home.

I'm sorry I've been ignoring the phone calls you made to me.

I'm sorry I talked back.

I'm sorry for fighting all the time.

I'm sorry you were landed with me for your daughter.

The more she thought about it, the more she couldn't look up.

Why did I go to university in Tokyo?

Why did I constantly complain like that?

Why did I say such horrible things and turn him away that day?

Regret was the only word that filled her mind. All she could pay attention to was Kengo staring at her like that.

He came all this way to see me, but as always, I'm not saying anything. He must be thinking I'm such an unadorable daughter.

Maybe it's time I go home.

I could make it all end by downing this coffee.

After all, there's nothing I could do that would help my father.

Michiko's hand tightened on the cup.

Just as it did . . .

'Michiko.'

Kengo looked into Michiko's face as he spoke to her.

'If by chance . . . something's troubling you . . . you know you can talk about it, right?'

He spoke in a choppy manner.

'You can talk to me about anything, you shouldn't have to worry about it alone . . . whatever it is . . . I want to be able to advise you.'

'What?'

'I may not be able to do it as well as your mother would have . . . But . . .'

Kengo looked up.

'But I still want you to tell me.'

She remembered. That look. It was a look that he had been giving her constantly, before and after her mother's death. He had not changed.

However, until that day, she had only seen him as being angry.

Do your homework.

Go to bed.

Don't stay up too late.

Choose your friends.

Don't wear those clothes.

Not that one.

I won't allow that.

On every occasion, he had been looking at Michiko with the same expression and the same feeling. Her perception of him as overbearing had been because her eyes were clouded. Her discomfort towards her father had entirely been the product of her clouded mind.

'Oh, um . . .'

I can't believe I didn't even realize that . . .

'Well, actually . . .'

I should talk about Yusuke. It probably will throw him for a loop. But if I want to tell him, it's now or never

'Dad, I er . . .'

'Hmm?'

'I'm pregnant.'

Michiko was staring at the coffee shaking in her cup. She

didn't know what expression was on Kengo's face. But his breathing was more excited and louder.

He's probably angry.

Putting herself in her father's shoes, she thought it only natural that he would be. Now she was twenty-five years old.

But from his perspective, it was only less than a year since she'd left her hometown and moved to Tokyo. He was hearing this confession from his daughter who was not yet twenty years old.

'He asked me to marry him . . .'

But I'll tell him all the same. About me now. I'll never see him again . . .

When Michiko looked up, Kengo appeared quite sad. His daughter had spread her wings and left the nest. Perhaps, from the moment he sent her off to Tokyo, Kengo had foreseen that such a day was not far off.

'I see,' he replied with a bitter feebleness.

He tried to smile, but the wrinkles between his eyebrows just furrowed more deeply, making him look angry. But that actually wasn't what Michiko wanted to tell him.

'But I'm scared.'

She couldn't stop her hands from shaking.

'I don't know if I deserve to be happy. I've said and done a lot of horrible things to you, Dad . . . Although you have always been looking out for me, rather than noticing I ignored you instead and said a lot of selfish things . . .' *I drove you away. If I hadn't turned you away at that time, maybe you wouldn't have died. I was only thinking of myself.* 'But still . . .'

'You shouldn't worry about that.'

Kengo interrupted her.

'I'm your father, I don't care if you swear at me, as long as you're fine. That's all that matters.'

'Dad.'

Large tears spilled from Michiko's eyes. Kengo looked at her and gave her a wry smile. He didn't know how to deal with his daughter's tears.

Then he said abruptly, 'Oh, here, take this . . .' as if to escape her gaze. He reached into his waist pouch, brought something out and held it out to her.

'I've been saving up to give it to you when you get married.'

It was a bankbook and a personal seal.

'I guess now is the right time,' he said with a broad smile.

'Oh, Dad . . .'

Beep, beep, beep, beep, beep . . .

The alarm went off.

'Oh . . .' Michiko gasped. Her eyes met the youthfully faced Kazu. Kazu didn't say anything. But she nodded slowly as if to confirm, it's time.

'Dad, I . . .'

'Don't worry, just be happy. It's the only thing that makes me happy.'

He was looking at Michiko kindly.

His face must have looked something like this when I was born.

Beep, beep, beep, beep, beep . . .

'I just need to go to the toilet . . .'

Kengo saw this alarm sounding as an opportunity to get up from his seat. He was wincing in embarrassment.

'Dad!'

As Kengo was on his way to the toilet, Michiko spontaneously called out to stop him.

This is my last time to say goodbye. But there's so much more to say.

'. . . Hmm?'

Kengo turned around.

'I . . .'

Michiko wiped away her tears and tried her best to smile.

'I'm glad I'm your daughter.'

Perhaps it looked like she was pulling a face, or not smiling very well. Still, she wanted to see her father off with a smile.

I'm sure Dad went to a lot of trouble to bring me my favourite takoyaki because he wanted to make me happy and see me smile. So, may my smiling face be his last image of me.

That was her deepest wish.

'Thank you.'

Kengo looked at Michiko's face, seemingly confused at what she had suddenly said. 'Oh,' he said, and while sniffing, headed out of the room to the toilet.

As soon as Kengo was out of sight, Michiko finished her coffee in one gulp. Immediately, she began to feel light and fluffy. Her surroundings started cascading down from the ceiling to the floor.

I'm returning – back to the present without my father.

Closing her eyes, she could still see Kengo's beaming face. She was able to make her father smile.

Thank heavens.

Michiko closed her eyes slowly.

The next thing Michiko knew, the woman in the white dress, who must have returned from the toilet, was standing right in front of her. From behind the counter, a waitress with long ponytailed hair was staring at her.

It was grown-up Kazu. Michiko had returned to the present.

'Move,' said the woman in the white dress, and Michiko surrendered her seat in a hurry.

She was not afforded the time for reveries.

When the woman in the white dress was seated, Kazu came carrying a tray with a new coffee for her.

'How was it?' Kazu asked as she cleared away the cup Michiko had used and served the cup for the woman in the white dress.

'I . . .'

CLANG-DONG

Just as Michiko was about to say something, the doorbell rang and Yusuke entered.

'Michiko.'

Standing some metres away from Michiko, his voice was

feeble. Michiko remembered that earlier that day, she said she would not be able to marry him.

Yusuke was keeping his distance, wary of those words she had spoken.

Don't worry, just be happy.

Her father's words rang in her ear.

She walked up to Yusuke's side, turned to Kazu and said, 'I think I want to be happy with this guy.'

That was her answer to Kazu's question 'How was it?' on her return from the past.

'What?'

Yusuke couldn't mask his surprise at Michiko's different attitude compared with earlier in the day.

'Oh, I see,' said Kazu, showing a faint smile.

'Yes. I'm sure that would make my father happy too . . .'

In her hand, she was gripping the bankbook she received from Kengo.

A phone could be heard ringing from the back room.

Michiko and Yusuke both nodded courteously to Kazu and left the cafe side by side.

CLANG-DONG

After the two had left, Nagare appeared from the back room cradling Miki. She had perhaps been grizzling, as her eyes were moist.

'Hey, remember Professor Kadokura?' Nagare asked Kazu.

It was past closing. Kazu was doing the finishing-up jobs.

She just needed to wash the dishes, give the floor a quick clean, and bring in the sign from outside.

'Yes,' she replied as she went into the kitchen.

While still cradling Miki, Nagare went outside to take in the sign. The only sound inside, empty except for the woman in the white dress, was the soft ticking of the pendulum clocks.

Kazu finished the dishes and Nagare returned with the sign.

'You were saying?'

'What's that?'

'About Professor Kadokura.'

'Oh, yeah.'

Nagare scratched his head in an exaggerated manner – not that he had forgotten.

'He rang up to say his wife had miraculously woken up . . .' he told Kazu.

'Oh, really?'

'Yeah.'

'Well, that's good news.'

'. . . Sure is.'

A moment later, Miki started swinging her fist-clenched arms. 'OOWAAAGGHH!' She began crying loudly.

'Oh, it's milk time, is it?'

'I'll get some ready.'

'Thanks, Kazu.'

As Kazu left for the kitchen, Nagare ambled over to the cash register while comforting Miki and picked up a photo placed next to it.

It showed the smiling face of Kei Tokita, Nagare's wife. She had died soon after giving birth to Miki. The seasons had continued to pass. Some people had come to this cafe and returned to the past. There were others who had not, still others who had left after hearing the rules.

'So fast. It's already been a year.'

Nagare gazed at the photo.

'Here you go.'

'Oh, thanks.'

Nagare returned the photo and took the bottle of formula from Kazu.

'She'll be all grown up before we know it. She'll grow up, and . . .'

'Yeah.'

Nestled in Nagare's arms, Miki began drinking. Gazing at this adorable scene, Kei inside the photo looked happy. That is how it appeared to Kazu, at any rate.

AUTHOR'S NOTE

This story is a work of fiction. It bears no relationship to people, shops, organizations, etc. in real life. The fourth chapter, 'The Daughter', however, was modelled on *One More Cup of Coffee?*, a radio drama written by the author on request by the radio programme *Date fm* (FM SENDAI) in Sendai, Miyagi Prefecture. It was broadcast on the seventh anniversary of the Great East Japan Earthquake on 11 March 2018.

Hailing from Ibaraki, Osaka Prefecture, Toshikazu Kawaguchi was born in 1971. Novelist, screenwriter and playwright, he won the tenth Suginami Drama Festival grand prize for the play *Before the coffee gets cold*. The namesake novel adaption was nominated for the Japan Booksellers Award in 2017, and a film adaption was made in 2018. He is active in theatres and YouTube as the face of Kawaguchi Productions. It is his dream to stage *Before the coffee gets cold* in all forty-seven prefectures across Japan. His hobbies are weight training, travel and hot springs, and his motto is 'live as you are'.

BEFORE THE COFFEE GETS COLD SERIES

More than 1 million copies sold worldwide

In a charming Tokyo cafe, customers are offered the unique experience of time-travel. But there are rules and the journey does not come without risks. Customers must return to the present before the coffee gets cold . . .

Translated from Japanese by Geoffrey Trousselot, Toshikazu Kawaguchi's heartwarming and wistful series tells the stories of people who must face up to their past in order to move on with their lives.

What would you do if you could travel back in time?